Constable David Maratse
Omnibus Edition #3

by Christoffer Petersen

CHRISTOFFER PETERSEN

Constable David Maratse
Omnibus Edition #3

Published by Aarluuk Press

Copyright © Christoffer Petersen 2019

Original Cover Image: Hubert Neufeld

ISBN: 978-87-93680-87-6

www.christoffer-petersen.com

Introduction

I grew up on Jack London's Arctic adventure stories, often reading by torchlight on school nights when I should have been sleeping. Stories about travelling by dog sledge kept me awake at night, and I dreamed of one day living in the Arctic. As I grew older, and read more and more stories, I made plans. I read everything I could about dog sledging, worked with Alaskan Huskies in Alta, Norway, Siberian Huskies in Thetford, England, and more Alaskans in Maine, USA. But it wasn't until I married a Dane, trained to be a teacher, and moved to Greenland, that I discovered the real ups and downs of Arctic life.

As a teacher I got to know the people of Greenland, their customs, traditions, passions, and beliefs. The children taught me just as much as I taught them. My job allowed me to see a lot of Greenland during the seven years I lived there, but my heart will forever be rooted in the sledge dog districts, as is Constable David Maratse's.

My last job in Greenland was as a teacher of English at the Police Academy in Nuuk, and it was the cadets and my colleagues who gave me access to their world. It was during this time that I learned even more about the challenges of police work in Greenland, and, equally, the rewards.

Maratse first appeared in my first book *The Ice Star* – a thriller set in Greenland. He reappeared in the second book: *In the Shadow of the Mountain*, and was mentioned in the third: *The Shaman's House*. But despite Maratse's quiet, steady character, he demanded, in his own taciturn way, a series of his own – he had stories to tell.

To get to know Maratse, I started writing short stories, to discover more about the man, and to give him a solid background to be developed in later books such as *Seven Graves, One Winter*, *Blood Floe*, and *We Shall Be Monsters*. I never intended to write more than a couple of stories, but four stories later and it seems that there is plenty more to tell.

The Greenland Crime stories do feature crimes, but they are bolted to the Greenland granite with stories that encapsulate the exciting and seemingly exotic culture of the Greenlandic people, their language, politics, and life in an often inhospitable land.

With every story I write, I bring Greenland that bit closer to home, to me, and, hopefully, to you too.

I hope you enjoy reading these stories as much as I enjoy writing them.

Chris
July 2018
Denmark

Scrimshaw

~ A short story of art and innocence in the Arctic ~

Part 1

Constable David Maratse thumbed the pages of his paperback, catching the individual sheets beneath his nail as he looked at the clock on the wall of the dentist's waiting room. He had started the book – a dog eared copy of Frank Herbert's *Dune* – on the flight from Kulusuk on the east coast of Greenland to the capital, Nuuk, on the west. The ice sheet he flew over reminded Maratse of the desert in the science fiction novel, both environments were equally dry and equally bright, just like the teeth in the posters framed on the waiting room walls. Maratse pressed his tongue against the tooth that was bothering him and immediately wished that he hadn't. He thumbed the pages again, nodding at a small boy sitting beside his mother, before leaning back in his chair and closing his eyes.

"David?" a woman said, as she stepped out of the surgery and scanned the patients waiting to see her.

The dentist liked first names only, Maratse remembered as he stood up, tucked the book inside his jacket pocket and walked across the room to the surgery. He shook the dentist's hand, mumbled something in agreement when she suggested he hang his jacket on the hook on the wall, and then sat down on the dentist's chair.

"I checked the records," Clara Matthiesen said. "It's been two years since your last check-up."

"*Iiji.*"

"And your doctor referred you?"

Maratse nodded.

"And now you're here." Clara smiled before putting on her mask. "Just relax, David. I'll take a look and then we can decide what needs to be done."

Maratse turned as Clara's assistant came into the room, and then he leaned back in the dentist's chair, closed his eyes and opened his mouth.

"You're still smoking, I see," Clara said, as she pricked Maratse's gums with the dental scaler. "And here we are. Yes, I can see why your doctor sent you. That tooth will have to come out."

Maratse opened one eye, nodded once, and then closed it again. He gripped his belt in both hands, as Clara and her assistant prepped him for the surgery, administering the anaesthetic, chatting all the way through the procedure, until Maratse's cheeks were drawn tight, as if he had just sledged twelve hours in minus thirty degrees. His face was stiff, and his tongue was thick as he swilled his mouth and spat bloody water into the bowl the assistant held for him.

"It will hurt for a few days," Clara said, as she pulled the mask from her face. "Can you stick around?"

"Why?"

"In case of infection. I'd like you to come back at the end of the week, before you go back east. Surely, you've got a few days leave?"

"I'll call Ittoqqortoormiit."

"Good," she said. "Oh, and if you're wondering what to do while you're here, then you should definitely go to

Katuaq, the cultural centre, later this afternoon. There's an exhibition of Tupilaq and other bone carvings. The artist will be there. He's getting an award. You should check it out. I think he's from Ittoqqortoormiit, also."

"What's his name?"

"Ah, just a minute. Let me see if I can find it," Clara said, as she checked her smartphone, scrolling through her mail, the tip of her short, rounded nail clacking on the screen. "I get *Katuaq*'s newsletter," she said. "Here we are. His name is Nappartuku Mikkiki."

"Tuku?" Maratse said, as he took his jacket from the hook on the wall.

"You know him?"

"We've met."

"Then you must go," Clara said. She checked her phone again. "Would you believe he's eighty-one?"

"*Iiji*," Maratse said. He shook the dentist's hand and walked out.

Maratse nodded at the little boy as he crossed the waiting room floor and opened the door to the street. He clumped down the wooden stairs and stepped onto the gritty road, scuffing tiny stones beneath his boots as he lit a cigarette. Maratse winced as the smoke curled into the new gap between his teeth at the back of his mouth, shrugged at the pain and clamped the cigarette between his lips. He stuffed his hands into his jacket pockets and walked towards the cultural centre. He thought about going into the police station opposite *Katuaq* to organise his leave, and then decided it could wait – they weren't expecting him before the following morning.

The exhibition poster in the window of the cultural centre caught Maratse's eye as he walked towards the door. He stopped in front of it, finished his cigarette and studied the fierce black eyes of *nanoq* – the polar bear – that Tuku had set inside the head of a creamy figure carved from the tooth of the narwhal. Lots of Greenlandic artists, mostly men, carved animals and the more grotesque Tupilaq from whale bone and reindeer antlers. Maratse had seen many fine examples, including those he had confiscated from tourists trying to take them out of the country. There was no problem with figures and jewellery made from antlers, soapstone, and wood, but whale and bear products were restricted under the CITES agreement, which Maratse grew tired of explaining to angry tourists at the airport.

"We weren't told," they would say, and, often, it was true.

"We want our money back," they would demand, only to be told that there was nothing to be done.

But Tuku's work, Maratse knew, was only sold in reputable gift shops, and mostly to Danes who, after living for a minimum of six months in Greenland, were allowed to take whale products back to Denmark. Tuku had a particular style, a signature tilt of the figure's head, and his name neatly scrawled on the base. His artistic eye, Maratse believed, came from the time Tuku had spent on the ice as a hunter. He could carve the raven's wing, as if the feathers brushed his face while he bent over the bone with the hobby drill. He had seen the polar bear roar, caught the huff of its rancid breath, and would capture the same in the figures he carved, his fingers stiff with age and a lingering cold, but not the slightest shake of the hand.

Maratse checked his watch, discovered he had an hour before Tuku was scheduled to speak, and found a seat at a table in the cultural centre's café. He ordered coffee, tugged his book from his pocket and started to read, ignoring the café's thick pine wood and glass interior in favour of fictive sands.

The worms of *Dune* tilted their heads as they broke the surface of the desert planet. Maratse drifted with them, absently reaching for his coffee, ignoring the ache in his gums as he sipped, letting his thoughts run wild with the idea of Tuku carving Tupilaq from the tooth of a desert worm. He put down the coffee mug and turned the page, only to pause as someone sat down at his table. Maratse lowered the book to his lap and smiled.

"Hello Piitalaat," he said.

"My name is still Petra," Petra said. "Or Constable Jensen."

"I like *Piitalaat*."

"I know," she said. "But, enough about that. Why are you here and why didn't you call?" Petra leaned back in her chair, pressing the collars of her police jacket flat against her shoulders, before crossing her arms over her chest.

"I only arrived this morning."

"But you knew you were coming."

"*Iiji.*"

"And still, you didn't call."

Petra's lips curled in one corner, dimpling her cheek as her eyes glistened. She started to laugh, and Maratse laughed with her.

"It's good to see you," he said.

"And you," she said. "But I still don't know why you are here."

"Dentist."

"Really?" Petra wrinkled her nose. "Was it bad?"

"It was like pulling teeth…" Maratse reached for his

coffee and hid his smile behind the lip of the mug.

"That was bad," Petra said, as Maratse nodded. "Well, bad jokes aside, are you here to see Nappartuku Mikkiki?"

"The dentist said I should."

"Oh, well if she said so…"

"And I've got nothing else to do."

Petra sighed. "Of course not. But then, if you'd called, we could have made plans. Then you wouldn't be bored."

"I didn't say I was bored," Maratse said. He lifted his book from his lap and slid it onto the table.

"And how many times have you read that one?" Petra held up her hand. "If it's more than once, I don't want to know." She pushed back her chair and stood up, curling loose strands of hair behind her ears as she waited for Maratse. "Come on," she said. "They're starting soon, and I don't want to miss Nivi's speech."

"Who?"

"Nivi Winther? She's the Minister for Education, Culture, Church and Foreign Affairs, but everyone knows she has a good chance of becoming Greenland's First Minister. I want to hear her talk."

"That's why you came?"

"Of course. I'm not *really* interested in Tupilaq. You should know that."

Maratse stood up and stuffed his book into his pocket. He walked beside Petra to the concert hall, glancing at her as she slipped her arm around his.

"What?" she said.

"Nothing."

"Maratse, you're on sick leave, and I'm off duty, and Gaba is on the other side of Nuuk right now, at a domestic."

"Gaba?"

"You remember Gaba Alatak? Leader of the SRU?" Petra said, as they stepped inside the concert hall and found two seats in one of the middle rows.

"I remember," Maratse said, as they sat down.

"Gaba and I are maybe seeing each other. I haven't decided yet." Petra leaned back in her seat and crossed her legs. "But never mind that. What about you? What have you done since Ilulissat?"

"Ilulissat?"

"When we caught the woman stealing the patterns?" Petra leaned forwards and turned her head to stare at Maratse. "Are you all right? Is it the anaesthetic? Or are you in pain?"

Maratse shrugged. "Maybe the anaesthetic," he said. "*And* the pain."

Petra took his hand and clamped it against her thigh.

"Well," she said. "I'll look after you now." She leaned back in her seat as an old man with a bent back shuffled onto the stage. He wore the white cotton smock and black trousers that men wear on formal occasions. The black leather cord around his neck held a large figure of a polar bear that sat flat against his chest. Against the white background of his smock, the bear looked like it could be crawling across sea ice, and Maratse leaned forwards for a better look.

"Is that him?" Petra asked.

"*Iiji*," Maratse said with a nod. He settled in his seat and Petra squeezed his hand.

"Here she comes," she said, pointing with her free hand. "That's Nivi. And you see the pretty young woman walking beside her? That's Tinka, her daughter."

"You know her?"

"I read about her in the paper. You do get *Sermitsiaq* in Ittoqqortoormiit, don't you?"

"I read books," Maratse said. "Not newspapers."

Petra sighed. "I give up. You're hopeless."

"I like the simple life," Maratse said. "Politics complicates things." He pointed at the old man standing beside Nivi Winther at the podium in the centre of the stage. "Tuku understands."

"And I don't?"

"I didn't say that, Piitalaat."

"I know," she said. "Anyway, shush now. It's starting."

Nivi Winther placed her notes on the podium in front of her as the last of the guests took their seats. She smiled up at the crowd, turning her head to take in the entire room, letting her gaze linger as she recognised different people in the audience.

"I've been cheeky today," she said, as the last few people took their seats. "I've taken the liberty of bringing my daughter with me. Tinka," she said, waving with a slender hand towards her daughter, "is on a visit from gymnasium in Aasiaat. I'm sure many parents among you, know how hard it is to be separated from their children, especially when they grow up, and leave the nest." Nivi paused to enjoy the ripple of soft laughter in the audience. "I'm sure you will also appreciate that even when our daughters and sons are home on a visit, they rarely look up from their smartphones, or their computers, unless they are hungry, or want to know why they don't have any more clean clothes."

"So true," Petra whispered, squeezing Maratse's hand and smiling as the people on either side of her laughed with Nivi Winther. Maratse frowned as he remembered that Petra had grown up in a children's home, but he let the thought go as Nivi continued.

"Imagine then how surprised I was when Tinka asked me if she could come with me today, when we celebrate the work of one of Greenland's greatest and most modest artists. You see, Tinka knows who Nappartuku Mikkiki is. And not just because she Googled his name from the poster on the way in."

Nivi paused again to allow for another ripple of laughter.

"I thought that might be the case. But it's not true. Tinka worked in a gift shop last summer, and she took an interest in the artwork on sale there, and so she discovered Nappartuku Mikkiki's work. She discovered one of Greenland's greatest talents, just like many tourists know the names of the artists who have carved the souvenirs they buy or painted the prints they have bought. As Minister for Greenland's Culture, I am excited to open the exhibition of Nappartuku's work, today, so that Greenlanders may come to know his art, and to better appreciate why his work has received such recognition and praise from visitors to our country. Nappartuku," Nivi said, turning to look at the old man standing beside her, "we're here today to recognise your contribution to the culture and living tradition of our country. Naalakkersuisut – the Government of Greenland, wants to thank you for acting as a softly-spoken ambassador, spreading the love and interest for Greenland in the memories that people take home with them, after spending a holiday here, or perhaps even just a short visit. Personally, I want to thank you for creating art so powerful that it can capture the interest of a teenage girl," Nivi said, as the audience laughed and clapped. "And I hope you'll forgive me for that small indulgence." Nivi took a step back from the podium, gesturing for Tuku to take a step forward. "Ladies and gentlemen," she said. "Please welcome, Nappartuku Mikkiki."

Part 2

Maratse and Petra walked through the exhibition, pausing at each of the figures and Tupilaq, small and large, carved into whale ribs and walrus tusks. Petra teased Maratse each time they stopped at a model of a hunter on a sledge. The tiny sledges had squares of reindeer skin tied with intricate knots to the wooden thwarts. Tuku had hidden one of the sledges inside the cave of a reindeer skull sawed in half, sheltering the hunter from the ornate bear, carved from the tooth of a narwhal, prowling outside.

"It's you," Petra said, each time they found a similar figure on display.

Maratse grunted and they moved on, pausing to take in a hunting scene carved in a flowing diorama that stretched from one walrus tusk to the other. The scene portrayed a great hunt beneath the northern lights carved into the skull above the tusks.

Petra leaned forwards to read the sign on the wall behind the skull. "*From a private collection*," she said. "It must be worth a fortune."

Maratse nodded, tilting his head to one side and resisting the urge to trace the route of the hunter, sledge and dogs with his finger.

"I have a date at the gym with Atii," Petra said. "Can we meet later? For dinner maybe? I'll cook."

"You'll cook?"

"I can cook," Petra said, frowning at the smile on Maratse's lips.

"Then I'd like to come for dinner," he said.

"Good. I'll call you later."

Maratse waited until Petra had gone, before slipping outside for a smoke. He leaned against the windows, his back to the exhibition poster, ignoring the pain in his gum but wondering if he should take something for it. Maratse checked his pockets, searching for loose tablets but finding only lengths of twine, a bullet casing from a .22 rifle, and a rusty ring of metal that might once have been part of a dog anchor, buried in the rock outside his home in Ittoqqortoormiit. He gave up searching for tablets as a young woman walked out of the cultural centre and asked him for a light. Maratse gave her a box of matches, nodding when she lit her cigarette and returned them.

"You're a policeman," she said in Greenlandic, pointing at his jacket.

"*Iiji.*"

The woman flashed a brief smile and switched to the east coast dialect. "My name is Fiia Mikkiki," she said. "I'm Nappartuku's granddaughter."

Maratse recognised the sharp cut of her chin that matched her grandfather's, together with her slim nose. Tuku wore it like a beak, giving him a hawkish expression, while Fiia's nose was smaller, almost lost between her long east Greenlandic cheeks. She had a pretty face framed with long black hair, but sad eyes, Maratse thought.

"Do you know *ata*?" she asked.

"We've met," Maratse said.

"Today?"

"*Eeqqi*. Not today."

"Can I tell you something, as a policeman?"

"I'm not on duty," Maratse said. "But you can tell me."

"I thought because you're wearing a police jacket..."

"It's a good jacket," he said, shrugging as he finished his cigarette.

Fiia paused to look around the parking area. She waited for an older Danish couple to walk past before continuing. "*Ata* is not happy. Something is wrong. But he won't tell me what it is."

Maratse waited, stuffing his hands into his jacket pockets as he listened.

"We came here a week ago. We're staying at the hotel," Fiia said, pointing in the direction of Hotel Hans Egede, stretching into the sky to the east of *Katuaq*. "Everyone has been so nice to *ata* and me. They really love his art, but still he is sad. Something has been bothering him, ever since we arrived. He's acting so strange."

"Strange?"

"Like he's scared," Fiia said. She looked down at the cigarette between her fingers, staring at it as if noticing it for the first time. "I don't know why I smoke," she said. "I don't like it much."

"Fiia," Maratse said. "Can you think of anything that might scare Tuku? Is he sick?"

"Not sick," she said, avoiding Maratse's eye. Her thick eyebrows bunched together as she frowned. "Just old."

Maratse waited for Fiia to say something more, but she fell silent, flicking the ash from the tip of her cigarette, watching it curl away in the wind that brushed the dust onto the cars and into the creases of their clothes.

"I don't know how I can help," Maratse said. "I can talk to him…"

"No," she said. "Then he would know I was worried. He wouldn't want that. But maybe if you could just… I don't know…" Fiia flicked her cigarette onto the gravel, grinding it beneath the sole of her boot. She tugged a pair of gloves from her pocket, dropping a creased business card onto the ground as she stuffed her hands inside the gloves. "September is colder in Nuuk," she said.

Maratse nodded. He pointed at the card on the ground, started to speak, but Fiia walked away, weaving between a group of tourists exiting the cultural centre before Maratse could stop her. He bent down to pick up the card, turning it in his fingers as he read the name of the shop printed on the front: *Northern Light Gifts & Souvenirs*. Maratse looked up and across the street. Most of Nuuk's shops, services, cafés and restaurants were clustered around the centre of the city. The gift shop was just across the street. Maratse tucked the card into his pocket and started walking.

He crossed the tiny bridge over the drainage ditch from the car park to the main road and turned west towards the sea, before crossing between a gap in the traffic and entering the gift shop. The familiar smell of cured sealskin leather and slightly musty furs prickled inside his nose, as he squeezed between the tourists filling the shop. Maratse walked between the glass cabinets on his way to the books on the shelf at the back. The glass doors shuddered and the figures on display rattled, as he walked along the uneven floorboards. Maratse squeezed into a corner by the shelf to study the books, curious as to why he chose to visit the shop, only to remind himself that there *was* something about Fiia that caught his attention, he just wasn't sure exactly what. But the card had led him this far, and he had nothing better to do with his time. He was, he realised, a tourist in his own country, lost in the capital of Greenland. It felt good to have something to do while he gave his gums time to heal.

The cabinet doors rattled for a second time as the tourists jockeyed for position in the line at the desk, brandishing their credit cards as they waited to pay. Maratse caught the last part of a sentence in English, as a deep-throated tourist voiced his annoyance when the shop assistant said he couldn't buy the figure he wanted.

"I've just been to the exhibition," the man said. "They told me I could buy the artist's work in your store. And you're telling me I'm not allowed."

"You can buy it," the assistant said, "but you're not allowed to take it out of the country."

"So, you'll take my money, but you won't let me take it out of the shop? Young lady, that makes no sense whatsoever."

"It's because it is made of whale bone," the assistant said. "If you'd like something made out of reindeer antler or wood…"

"Listen, honey, we've got plenty of trees back home. If I wanted something made of wood, I could go down to the gift store on Main Street. But I'm here, in Greenland, and my wife and I want a souvenir."

"Then perhaps something in reindeer…"

"Does that guy from the exhibition have something made out of reindeer?"

"Erm, I don't think so."

"Don't think so? I *know* so. We read it on a card in

the exhibition. He only carves in whale or walrus. Is this whale or walrus?" the man asked, pressing the figure into the assistant's hand.

"Both are restricted under the CITES agreement…" she said.

"So, I can't buy either?"

"No. I'm afraid not."

"What kind of a backward country is this?" The man raised his voice. He turned to look at the tourists behind him. "Put your cards away folks. They won't let you buy anything, anyway." He turned back to the assistant, and said, "What's the point in having an exhibition for an artist, then telling us we can't buy his work? Eh?"

"We don't have anything to do with the exhibition," the assistant said.

"You don't have to tell me that. Now, do you have a manager? Or maybe the owner is around someplace?"

"She can't help you. It's the law…"

"We'll see about that," the man said.

Maratse slipped out of the gap between the bookshelf and the wall and walked quietly around the cabinets to the back of the line. One of the tourists turned as he bumped her shoulder. She looked at the police emblem stitched to his jacket and frowned.

"I'm a car park attendant," Maratse said in English, and smiled.

"Oh," she said, and turned away.

Maratse stepped to one side, behind a tall man, as a middle-aged woman came out of the office to deal with the tourist at the desk.

"Are you the owner?" the man asked.

"I'm Kista Sianiali," she said. "It's my shop."

"Are *you* going to sell me something?"

"I'd like to."

"But will you?" he asked. "Or will you start talking about the *sights* or whatever it is."

"You mean CITES, I think," Kista said. She lowered her voice and gestured for the man to follow her a few steps away from the desk. Maratse stepped around the tourists to listen in. "You need a CITES certificate for certain items," she said. "But there is a way for you to buy things, for a price, of course."

"Lady, I just want one of these figures, real bad. I'll pay your price. I can pay you right now."

"But not by card," Kista said. "Are you staying in a hotel?"

"The Hans Egede," the man said. "That's right. What about it?"

"Well, if we agreed on a price, then you could arrange to withdraw that amount on your card at the hotel, and then you could pay in cash."

"Pay you?"

"No, not me. But I have an associate who will help you."

"And I can buy this figure?" the man said, raising the Tupilaq he held in his hand.

"Not that one, but I guarantee it will be an original work by the artist."

"Well, that sounds fair."

"How long are you staying in Nuuk?"

"We leave at the end of the week."

"If you'll give me your name…"

"Malcolm Keenly," the man said.

"Perfect. I'll have someone contact you at the hotel. He'll leave a message at the front desk." Kista held out her hand and the man placed the Tupilaq in her palm.

"You're sure it will be as fancy as that one?"

"Quite sure," Kista said. She smiled as the man nodded and walked out of the shop.

Maratse followed, slipping around the tourists as he made his way to the door. He caught Kista's eye and she stopped him with a hand on his arm.

"What can I do for you, Constable?" she asked, in English. Maratse frowned, and Kista switched to Greenlandic. "Just browsing?"

"*Iiji*," Maratse said.

"So, there's nothing I can help you with?"

"Not today."

Maratse walked around Kista and out of the shop. He clumped down the steps and onto the side of the road, spotting the tourist as the man walked towards the hotel. Maratse hesitated for a moment, wondering if he should talk to the man, or go back to the exhibition to find Tuku. He waited until the tourist disappeared around the corner, and then walked back to the exhibition. He stopped at the information desk and asked where he could find Tuku, only to discover that the artist had left the exhibition just half an hour earlier.

"Hmm," Maratse said. He nodded his thanks and walked back to the street.

Technically, Maratse was off duty, but a policeman is never off duty, not really. He checked the time on his watch, and then walked towards the police station. It was too late to complete the paperwork to extend his sick leave, but he might just find a Constable interested in following up on the black market CITES deal. He could worry about Tuku Mikkiki in the morning.

Part 3

Petra scrolled through the playlist on her smartphone as she stirred the tomato sauce, settling on Simon and Garfunkel, for the *old man in the room*. Thirteen years older, she remembered. She flashed Maratse a cheeky smile as the opening bars of *Mrs Robinson* spilled out of her wireless speakers. Petra stopped stirring to tuck her wet hair into a knot, before boiling water for the pasta. Maratse sat in the armchair next to the glass window running the length of Petra's apartment. The late September sky filled with drifting curtains of greens and blues, as the Northern Lights spread above the rectangular body of water between Qinngorput and the city of Nuuk. Maratse sipped his coffee and let his book slip down his chest as he watched Petra cook in the kitchen.

"I heard you were at the station today," she said.

"*Iiji.*"

"Well?"

Maratse shrugged as Petra turned to look at him, pointing with a wooden spoon. She cursed as sauce dripped off the spoon and onto the wooden floor. Maratse waited as she cleaned up the mess, tossed the cloth into the sink and leaned on the counter.

"I asked for a bit of help," he said.

"You could have asked me," Petra said.

"You don't know what it is."

"No, but I would have helped."

Maratse put his coffee mug on the coaster on the windowsill, slid his book alongside it, and walked into the kitchen area. "It was about CITES and selling narwhal Tupilaq to tourists."

Petra wrinkled her nose. "You're right, I don't want anything to do with that. Lots of paperwork."

"That's the problem," Maratse said. "I think they are selling gifts without the proper papers."

"It won't be the first time," Petra said. "But who is *they* and why are you so interested all of a sudden?"

Maratse told Petra about the tourist in the gift shop. He showed her the business card, and then said, "But that's not why I'm interested."

"Why then?"

"Because Tuku's granddaughter said she's worried about him."

"See," Petra said, as she dialled down the heat under the pan of pasta. The water frothed over the side of the pan and spat on the hob. "That makes more sense. I was waiting for the human angle."

"Human angle?"

"Yes," she said. "There's always a human angle with you. I mean, you love nature, the sea especially, but no matter how much you try to hide it, you have a blind spot when it comes to people." Petra grinned as she pressed cork mats into Maratse's hands. "For the table," she said, pointing at the small dining table between the cooker and the couch.

Maratse placed the mats in the centre of the table, found cutlery in the draw and plates in the cupboard.

Petra nodded at the glasses cupboard as she stirred the sauce, wrinkling her nose as she scraped at the burnt layer at the bottom of the pan.

"I bought some wine," she said. "A treat."

Maratse swapped the water glasses for the two wine glasses at the back of the cupboard. Petra placed the food on the table, opened the wine, and lit a candle before sitting down at the table.

"I forgot to buy bread," she said, as Maratse sat down.

They barely spoke while eating, content in the silence that typically bothered Danes when invited to eat with Greenlandic families. Maratse nodded when Petra offered him more wine, smiling at the rosy glow spreading through Petra's cheeks. She filled his glass, then frowned as the knot in her hair slipped, releasing more wayward strands of jet-black hair, still damp, shining in the candlelight.

"Tell me about Nivi Winther," he said, as they finished eating.

"Tell me about the food first," she said.

"It was good, Piitalaat. *Qujanaq*."

Petra smiled, sipped her wine, and told Maratse why she liked Nivi Winther, and why Nivi would make a good First Minister.

"Because she doesn't discriminate," Petra said, tapping her finger on the table. "She speaks three languages…"

"So do you," Maratse said.

"Yes, but not my own. She speaks Greenlandic, but it's not an issue for her what you or I speak. She sees language as a means of communication, of sharing ideas, of agreeing, or even disagreeing with one another, so long as we are communicating." Petra paused to undo the knot in her hair, giving up the struggle and letting her hair fall onto her shoulders. "She could even communicate with you, Maratse," Petra said.

"Hmm," Maratse said, and reached for his wine.

"Exactly." Petra giggled. She lifted the bottle of wine and turned it in the light to see how much they had drunk. "On a work night," she said. "You're a bad influence."

"*Imaqa.*"

"Ah, so you admit it?" Petra put the bottle down and pointed her finger at Maratse. "Bad influence. Bad Maratse."

"Piitalaat," Maratse said.

"Yes?"

"You're drunk."

Petra giggled. "I know," she said, leaning her head to one side. A strand of hair slipped over her eyes and she stared through it. "David," she said.

"*Iiji?*"

"Take me to bed."

Maratse pressed his fingers around the wine glass. He took a sip, catching Petra's eye as she stared at him through a thin veil of wet black hair. A scratch of gravel outside in the parking lot scraped at the window. A raven croaked from the roof of the tower block next to Petra's. Maratse finished his wine. Petra turned the bottom of her glass with slow, clumsy fingers, watching Maratse. Waiting.

"You're like Nivi," she said, her voice low, her breath barely stirring the candle flame between them. "You don't judge. You don't expect. You don't…"

"What?" Maratse said, as he tipped the last of the wine from the bottle into his glass.

"Demand anything."

"Not from you, Piitalaat."

"But you're not going to sleep with me, are you?"

"*Eeqqi*," he said, and sipped his wine.

"Is there someone else? A woman waiting for you in a tiny house in Ittoqqortoormiit?"

Maratse shook his head.

"There's no-one?"

"Not yet," he said.

Petra smiled. "Okay." She took a long breath and clasped the edge of the table. "Okay, I might need a little help."

Maratse pushed his chair back from the table and walked around it. He slid his arm around Petra's back as she turned towards him. He pulled her gently to her feet, and she pressed her hands against his chest.

"Ready?" he asked.

"Just one minute more," she said.

Maratse felt Petra's wet hair on his chin as she pressed her head against his shoulder. He slid his hands higher up her back, pressing his nose into her hair as she swayed on her feet, just a little, just enough, so that the room was like the deck of a ship, drifting across the Labrador Sea beneath a swathe of soft lights.

"Piitalaat," Maratse said, as she started to snore softly in his arms.

Maratse picked her up, bumping her feet against the back of the chair and again on the door frame, as he carried her to her bedroom. He leaned to one side to pull the duvet across the bed, before laying her on the sheet and pulling the duvet back over her body.

"Five o'clock," she mumbled, as he brushed her hair from her forehead.

"What?"

"Set my alarm for five," she said, eyes closed, a soft smile on her lips. "Leave the dishes. Let yourself out."

Maratse sat on the side of Petra's bed, as he fiddled with the alarm clock on her bedside table. She tugged her hand out from under the duvet and patted his thigh.

"I usually use my phone."

"But I don't know how," Maratse said, as he flicked the alarm switch to the on position.

"Of course, you don't." Petra said. She opened her eyes and they shone in the light creeping in from the street lamps outside. "Your head is full of snow and ice," she said. "The simple life."

"I like it."

"I know."

Petra smiled as Maratse took her hand. He held it until she closed her eyes, letting go as she started to snore. Maratse closed the bedroom door on his way out, tidied the kitchen and cleaned the dishes. He turned off the lights and locked the door on his way out, zipping his jacket as he walked down the stairs.

Maratse lit a cigarette as he left Petra's apartment block. He smoked on his way to the bus stop opposite the school at the bottom of the hill, below the five apartment blocks of Qinngorput. He took the bus into the centre of Nuuk, getting off outside Hotel Hans Egede. Maratse checked the time before climbing the steps into the hotel and asking for Nappartuku Mikkiki.

"Is it official business?" the night manager asked, as he looked at Maratse's jacket.

"Yes," Maratse said.

The night manager nodded, pressing the handset to his ear as he dialled Tuku's room. Maratse leaned on the counter and rubbed his face with his hand. He could still smell Petra's hair on his fingers. His lips creased into a smile at the thought of her drinking a little too much on a work night. He pushed the other thoughts to one side, as the night manager lowered the handset.

"I'm sorry. There's no answer. Do you want me to send someone to his room?"

"No," Maratse said. "But maybe you could try his granddaughter, Fiia Mikkiki? She's also staying here."

Maratse waited, lifting his head suddenly as the night manager spoke with Fiia on the phone.

"She's coming down," he said, and pointed at the soft chairs by the window. "You can wait over there."

"*Qujanaq*," Maratse said, as he walked across the lobby to the chairs.

Fiia stepped out of the elevator shortly after Maratse sat down. Her shoulders shook as she walked over to him. She wiped her eyes with the backs of her hands, and then collapsed against Maratse's chest as he stood up to greet her.

"He's gone," she said. "He never came back from the exhibition. I don't know where he is."

"You've tried his room?" Maratse asked, as he gently prised Fiia away from his chest.

"Lots of times, and again when they called, just now." Fiia swallowed. She let Maratse guide to her the chair, clutching her arms around her stomach as she sat down. "No answer. His room is empty."

"You have a key?"

Fiia nodded.

"May I borrow it?"

Fiia tugged the credit card key out of her pocket and slid it across the table to Maratse.

"It's the on the fourth floor," she said. "Room 412."

"Will you stay here?"

"Yes."

"I'll be right back."

Maratse turned the key in his hand as he took the elevator to the fourth floor. He had locked his utility belt and service pistol in the cupboard at the station in Ittoqqortoormiit, and the lack of the weight pulling at his hips was notable in its absence. He stuffed his hands into his jacket pockets as the elevator doors opened. Maratse stepped out of the elevator and walked down the corridor to Tuku's room. He knocked twice, then pressed the key into the slot in the door, pausing for a second as he wondered if he should be wearing gloves.

Suicide did not discriminate between age and sex. It occurred to Maratse that a sad old man might choose to end his life in a strange room in a strange city, regardless of the accolades he had received for his work, perhaps even because of them.

Maratse called out Tuku's name as he stepped into the room. He checked the bed first, before pressing his fingers against the bathroom door, and opening it, slowly, as he pressed the card into the slot by the door and turned on the light.

The bath was empty, and there was no sign of blood or a struggle. The bathroom looked as if it might never have been used. Maratse exhaled, scanned the few personal items by the sink, and then returned to the bedroom.

The bed was made, and the top sheet was smooth. Maratse checked the bathroom again, found the triangle fold of the top layer of toilet paper on the hook, saw the neat row of towels hanging on the rack. The rubbish bins in the bathroom and the bedroom were empty. And, apart from an old jacket hanging on the back of the chair at the desk, there was no sign of anyone staying in the room.

Maratse checked under the bed, opened all the drawers and the wardrobe, and then pulled the key card from the slot before leaving and locking the room.

Tuku was gone. Lost in the city.

Part 4

Maratse woke to the sound of seagulls and motors. The Nuuk Seamen's Home had less stars than Hotel Hans Egede, but the location, and the price suited Maratse. Excessive comfort was not something that had ever bothered him; a good firm bed was all that he needed, and food to suit his palate. He ate breakfast in silence, nodding at the familiar faces of the guests seated at the tables around him, smiling at the thought of the last meal he ate before breakfast, wondering if Petra woke when her alarm rang, knowing that she did, she always did.

He took the bus into the centre of town and walked to the police station, kicking the grit from his boots on the stairs before opening the door and walking inside. Petra's desk was on the first floor. Maratse climbed the stairs, nodding at the police officers who passed him on the way down. He found Petra sitting at her desk, her smartphone pressed to her ear, and a bottle of water in her hand. She smiled at Maratse and nodded at the seat by the side of her desk, as she finished her call.

"Everything all right?" she asked, as she slid her phone onto the table and took a sip of water.

"I'm fine."

"Really? Something's on your mind." Petra leaned forwards and lowered her voice. "Did I embarrass you last night? I'm sorry if I did. It was a fun day. I had some wine…"

"Piitalaat," Maratse said.

"Yes?"

"Tuku is missing."

"The artist? You're sure now?"

"*Iiji*. I went to his hotel last night. His room was empty, apart from one jacket. His granddaughter doesn't know where he is. I want to report him missing." Maratse paused to unzip his jacket. "You have the Missing Persons desk."

"Yes, I do," Petra said. She pulled her notebook out of the cargo pocket on her trousers. "Normally we wait forty-eight hours for an adult, just to allow for travel time. You're sure he hasn't returned to Ittoqqortoormiit? You said the room was empty. No case?"

"Only his jacket."

"We can check the passenger manifest with Air Greenland." Petra paused, tapping the tip of her pen on the page.

"I can do that," Maratse said. "If you're busy."

"No," she said. "I want to help. But I have a meeting this morning." She checked her phone. "Right now, actually. I can call Air Greenland after that." Petra stood up and pulled her jacket from the chair, slipping her arms inside the sleeves as she looked at Maratse. "I have to go. I'm sorry."

"It's okay."

"David," she said. "I had a lovely night."

"*Iiji*."

She leaned closer and whispered in his ear, "Thanks for putting me to bed." A burst of colour rushed to Maratse's cheeks, and Petra smiled. "And here's me thinking you were immune to the wily charms of young female police officers."

"Not immune," Maratse said. "Just…"

"Don't." Petra said. "Just leave it at that. I have to go." Petra grabbed her notebook from the desk and straightened her hair. "I'll call you later," she said, as she brushed past Maratse and into the corridor.

Maratse asked the policeman at the next desk where the administration office was, thanked him, and followed his directions along the hall, only to be stopped by a young Danish officer on his way up the stairs.

"You're Maratse?"

"*Iiji.*"

"From East Greenland?"

"Yes."

"You came in yesterday," the officer said, checking his notes. "Something about CITES certificates?"

Maratse nodded.

"I have a name for you: Aqqaluk Sivertsen. He's twenty years old. Lives in Blok 23B, apartment 206. I think it's down by the water."

"I know where it is," Maratse said, taking the note as the young Danish police officer tore it from his notepad.

"I'm not sure about the details, but apparently this man is connected to the sale of whale products. He's quite low on the food chain, as far as we're aware."

"*Qujanaq,*" Maratse said.

He stuffed the note into his pocket as the Dane jogged back down the stairs. Maratse ducked into the administration office and signed the necessary form to extend his sick leave, answering with a shrug when the clerk asked him what he was going to do in Nuuk while he waited.

"Museums," Maratse said, on his way out of the door.

He walked to Blok 23B, hands tucked inside his jacket pockets, a cigarette in the corner of his mouth. The apartment blocks, like the infamous Blok P, were built in the '60s by the Danish government keen to modernise and urbanise the Greenlanders, encouraging them to move from the tiny coastal settlements to the city. Like any concrete apartment block built in that era, function was weighted higher than form. Blok 23B was no different. Maratse finished his cigarette, checked the name and number on the note, and walked inside.

The corridors were dark with black walls scrawled with '70s graffiti pushing for Greenlandic independence. Maratse's boots echoed dully as he climbed the stairs. He checked the numbers on the doors, ignored the jeers he received from a couple of drunks camped outside an open door, stepping around them as he walked the last few steps to number 206. Maratse tucked the note into his pocket and knocked on the door.

He checked his watch, wondering if Fiia Mikkiki would call him as they had agreed, the second she heard from Tuku. And then the door opened, and a young man with a wispy beard and black shoulder-length hair, glared at Maratse.

"Aqqaluk Sivertsen?" Maratse asked.

"*Aap.*"

"Can we talk?"

Aqqaluk paused to look around Maratse, checking the corridor on both sides, before stepping back inside the apartment. Maratse smiled, stuffing his foot inside the door as Aqqaluk tried to slam it shut.

"I just want to ask you a couple of questions,"

Maratse said.

Aqqaluk kicked the door once, then turned and ran.

All the apartments in Blok 23B were the same. A short entrance with a direct path to the terraced balcony at the back. Each apartment was linked, allowing neighbours to slip over the balcony when visiting. It was quicker than using the front door. Aqqaluk burst through the door to his balcony, kicked a garden chair out of the way, and climbed over the wall to his left, crashing through his neighbour's washing line as he ran to the next balcony.

Maratse followed, scrambling over the wall, ducking under the line of wet clothes and climbing over the next wall, and the next, as they ran the length of Blok 23B. Aqqaluk tried each door on every balcony, until he found one that was unlocked. Maratse heard the shouts as Aqqaluk burst into the apartment. He heard a woman's scream and caught a glimpse of Aqqaluk pushing her out of the way as he ran for the front door. Maratse pounded after him and slid into the corridor, bouncing off the door of the apartment opposite, before finding his feet and chasing Aqqaluk down the stairs to the street.

Aqqaluk raced straight into the road, slipping on the gravel and swerving around a dark blue police Toyota, as the driver slammed on the brakes. Maratse chased after him, slowing for a second to acknowledge the driver as he wound down the window.

"Gaba," Maratse said.

"What's going on? We had a call about a disturbance."

"I'm the disturbance," Maratse said, resting against the side of the patrol car, catching his breath.

"That's Aqqaluk Sivertsen," Gaba said, stabbing his

finger towards Aqqaluk as the young Greenlander slid over the rocks and out of sight. "What's he done?"

"Maybe nothing. But he ran."

Gaba leaned out of the car window and looked up at the residents of Blok 23B crowding the balconies above them. Some shouted, others swore, one woman tossed a beer bottle onto the street. Gaba reached for the radio mounted on the dashboard and called for backup, nodding for Maratse to get in.

"Where's your radio?" he asked as Maratse climbed into the passenger seat.

"Ittoqqortoormiit."

"And your pistol? Your belt?"

"I'm off duty," Maratse said.

"Really? And what are you doing?"

"Museums." Maratse grinned.

"Right."

Gaba rubbed his chin as he studied Maratse. The hairs of Gaba's goatee were trimmed in thin lines, neat and tidy, just like his meticulously shaved head. Maratse's heart slowed to a more acceptable beat as he waited for Gaba to speak. A second bottle smashed on the road in front of the patrol car. Gaba leaned out of the window and stared at the Greenlanders on the balconies. Slowly, they retreated, until just their heads were visible, as they stood on tiptoes, peeping over the wall at the spectacle below.

"They know me, and I know them," Gaba said, with a sigh. "But *you* got them all riled up. What's it all about? Why are you chasing Aqqaluk Sivertsen?"

"I'm looking for Nappartuku Mikkiki. The artist."

"What kind of artist?"

"Scrimshaw – he carves bone, Tupilaq…"

"Okay, I get it. *That* kind of artist. You say he's missing?"

"*Iiji.*"

"And you think Aqqaluk knows where he is?"

"*Imaqa*," Maratse said. "He's the only lead I've got."

"What lead?"

"Tuku's granddaughter dropped a business card from a gift shop. The gift shop owner made a deal with a tourist to sell Tupilaq without a CITES certificate. I got Aqqaluk's name from the station."

"And they know you're working a case – off duty?"

"It's not a case. I'm just looking for Tuku."

"Maratse," Gaba said. "Don't get smart. You're in the city now. You're on leave."

"To visit the dentist."

"And when do you go back?"

"After a check-up, at the end of the week."

"And you thought you'd amuse yourself until then?" Gaba laughed. "I can see why Petra likes you," he said. "But for a simple cop from the settlements, you certainly know how to have a good time."

"This is not entertainment, Gaba. A man is missing. I'm trying to find him."

"All right," Gaba said, as he shifted the Toyota into gear. "Let's go find your man and you can ask your questions." The wail of approaching sirens turned Gaba's head. He nodded at the police officer sitting in the passenger seat as a second patrol car pulled alongside.

"Everything all right?"

"We're fine," Gaba said. "Just helping out a colleague from Ittoqqortoormiit." Gaba jerked his thumb at Maratse. "If you sit here for a minute, we're just going to pick someone up."

Gaba waved as he pulled away, driving along the edge of the road as Maratse scanned the rocks below.

"There's a narrow path down there," Gaba said. "If he's taken that, he can get all the way to *Saqqarliit* then double back into the city centre. Of course, he might hide and wait, but I don't think so."

"Why not?"

"Aqqaluk likes to run." Gaba grinned. "It's what he usually does."

The Toyota's wheels spun on the grit on the side of the road as Gaba accelerated. He turned onto *Saqqarliit* and then flicked on the emergency lights and the siren as he spotted Aqqaluk running up the road ahead of them. He pulled alongside the young Greenlander, slowing to match Aqqaluk's pace.

"Why are you running, Aqqa?" Gaba asked.

"That crazy policeman chased me," he said, pointing at Maratse, as he slowed to a stop.

Gaba turned off the siren and stopped the patrol car, nodding for Maratse to get out, as he opened the driver's door and clapped his hand on Aqqaluk's shoulder.

"I want to ask you two questions," Maratse said, as he walked up to Aqqaluk.

"And he'll answer them," Gaba said. "Won't you, Aqqa?"

"I don't have to."

"Don't say that, Aqqa." Gaba increased his grip, turning Aqqaluk towards the side of the Toyota and pressing him against the rear passenger door. Aqqaluk squirmed in his grasp, then turned his head to look at Maratse, nodding once.

"Do you know Nappartuku Mikkiki?" Maratse asked.

Aqqaluk frowned, as he glanced at Gaba.

"Just answer the question, Aqqa."

"*Aap*, I know him."

"Do you know where he is?"

"Why should I know where he is?"

Aqqaluk groaned as Gaba tightened his grip.

"See, that's not an answer," Gaba said. "Do you know where he is?"

"*Naamik*."

"Why am I not convinced?" Gaba looked at Maratse. "That's two questions. Mind if I ask another?"

"Go ahead."

Maratse tucked his hands into his jacket pockets, as Gaba spun Aqqaluk around to face him. Gaba jabbed two thick fingers into Aqqaluk's chest, pinning him to the car.

"You and I know each other," he said. Gaba waited for Aqqaluk to nod, before he continued. "And we both know who pulls your strings. So, my question is, if you don't know where Nappartuku is, who does?"

"I don't know," Aqqaluk said. He flinched as Gaba stabbed his chest with his fingers.

"Come on, Aqqa. Just say the name. Unless you want me to say it? Is that easier?"

Aqqaluk nodded.

"Okay then, we'll do it your way." Gaba paused for a second, and then said, "Qaqi Valerius. Does *he* know where Nappartuku is?"

"*Aap*," Aqqaluk said. He looked at Maratse, and added, "He knows. It's him you should talk to."

Gaba sighed. He patted Aqqaluk's chest and nodded for him to go.

"Well, Maratse," Gaba said, as he watched Aqqaluk run back towards the apartment block. "This isn't good, not good at all. Maybe you would be better off visiting a museum."

"But you know Qaqi Valerius, and you know where he is?" Maratse asked.

"Yeah. I know him, and I know exactly where he is."

Part 5

They passed Aqqaluk on the street as Gaba drove back to the police station. Gaba parked close to the entrance, tapping Maratse's arm and gesturing for him to wait as he turned in his seat.

"Qaqi is a tricky customer," Gaba said. "He uses people like Aqqaluk, cutting them loose at the first sign of trouble. If you want to talk to Qaqi, you have to have more than just questions. You need to force him to listen, and you need to have something concrete to grab his attention."

"Hmm," Maratse said. "What do you suggest?"

Gaba pointed at the gift shop on the other side of the street. "You said she's selling CITES protected souvenirs without a certificate?"

"*Iiji.*"

"That fits with what we've heard about Qaqi Valerius. If the owner gives us a link to him – officially, not just something you overheard, then we've got enough to go and talk to Qaqi."

"Today?"

Gaba checked his watch. "Yeah, today. I've got a training session scheduled with the SRU, we'll just make it a *live* training session." Gaba grinned as Maratse stared at him. "Yes, Maratse, I'm going to task the SRU to come with you when you talk to Qaqi. He's *that* kind of guy."

Gaba turned at a knock on the window. He rolled it down and Petra leaned into the patrol car.

"It's official," she said. "Tuku's granddaughter just reported him as missing."

"She came to you?" Maratse asked.

"Just twenty minutes ago." Petra tugged her notebook out of her pocket. "There's something else," she said. "After your run in with Aqqaluk Sivertsen this morning, the Commissioner finds it hard to believe that you are on sick leave." Maratse exchanged a look with Gaba as Petra continued. "He's taken an interest in the case, and has decided, despite his better judgement," Petra said, pausing as a smile played across her lips. "He *said* that he's going to ignore your behaviour, this time, but insists you work closely with your colleagues from Nuuk."

"My colleagues," Maratse said.

"Me," Petra said, turning the notebook to show Maratse her notes. "The Commissioner's words, my punctuation."

"That's settled then," Gaba said. He tapped Petra on the arm and pointed at the gift shop. "If you take our East Greenland friend shopping for souvenirs, I will get Miki and the crew ready."

"What's SRU got to do with this?" Petra asked.

"Qaqi Valerius," Gaba said. "Maratse will fill you in."

"*He's* involved with this?"

"There's a good possibility."

Petra stepped back as Gaba opened the driver's door. Maratse climbed out of the passenger seat. The wind tugged at his thick black hair as he walked around the back of the patrol car. Gaba stopped him and opened the boot.

"You're not properly dressed, Constable," he said, tugging a utility belt out of the back of the Toyota. "No pistol, but I don't like you walking around naked," he said, with a glance at Petra. "So, extendable baton, pepper spray, cuffs and flashlight. The usual." He handed the belt to Maratse. "I'll feel a little better if you put it on, and even more if you promise to wait for backup the next time you want to question someone."

"Okay," Maratse said, as he buckled the utility belt around his waist. Petra hid a smile behind her notebook as Gaba perfected his scowl.

"And you," Gaba said.

"Me?" Petra tapped her chest with the corner of the notebook, her eyes wide as she played the innocent party. "I'm the one who just talked to the Commissioner."

"Right, just delivering orders. Just keep Maratse out of trouble."

"Of course."

"And that doesn't mean a candlelit dinner for two," Gaba said, adding another crease to the scowl across his brow.

"You heard about that?" Petra said, as blood rushed to her cheeks. She risked a quick glance at Maratse, took a breath, and composed herself. "You're the one who has trouble committing, Gaba. Perhaps if you hadn't blown me off the other night…"

Maratse coughed. He tucked his hands into his pockets, waited for Gaba and Petra to notice him, and then nodded at the gift shop.

"It closes at lunch," he said. "We should go now."

Gaba shut the Toyota's boot, locking the patrol car with a click of the key fob. He pointed at the station, and said, "I'll be inside. The team will be here in an hour. You've got until then to get the proof we need to talk to Qaqi." He walked away, slipped his finger inside the ring of keys, and spun the fob around his finger as he marched into the police station.

"Sorry," Petra said, as soon as Gaba was inside the building.

"It's okay," Maratse said. He turned towards the gift shop and started walking. Petra fell in step beside him.

"He's so arrogant," she said.

"*Iiji.*"

"And his ego is bigger than Greenland."

Maratse nodded.

"But his body, well…"

"Piitalaat…"

"Yes," she said. "Sorry."

Maratse stopped at the side of the road, nodded at the gift shop, and told Petra what had happened after he left her desk earlier that morning.

"And you think the owner…"

"Kista Sianiali," Maratse said.

"You think she'll give us Qaqi?"

"*Imaqa*, but we're going to try," he said, as they crossed the road. "Follow my lead."

"Sounds interesting." Petra resisted the urge to slip her hand through Maratse's arm and followed him inside the gift shop.

The glass doors of the cabinets rattled as Maratse pushed his way gently through the small group of tourists shopping for souvenirs. He worked his way to the desk and asked the assistant to fetch Kista.

"Is she in trouble?" the assistant asked.

"Not yet," Maratse said.

Petra frowned at Maratse, as soon as the assistant went into the office.

"What are you going to do?" she whispered.

Maratse shrugged. His lips creased into a smile, but he straightened his face as soon as Kista stepped out of the office and approached the desk. Maratse pressed his hands on the counter and spoke in English.

"I was here yesterday," he said.

"I remember," Kista said. "But you couldn't speak English yesterday."

"I'm a quick learner."

"I see." Kista looked at the tourists, and then asked if they could continue in Greenlandic.

"Danish," Maratse said. He pulled his notebook out of his pocket and made a show of turning the page. "Yesterday, you talked with a tourist called Malcolm Keenly," he said.

"Yes?"

"I overheard you."

Kista glanced at Petra, before nodding. "I know." She waited as Maratse shut his notebook, and then said, "Nothing happened. There's no proof, apart from what you think I might have said. No-one has contacted Keenly. There's nothing illegal going on." Kista crossed her arms over her chest.

"Not yet," Maratse said. "But what you don't know is that Mr Keenly is an Enforcement Officer with the Convention on International Trade in Endangered Species."

"He's undercover," Petra said. "And liaising with the Greenland Police in Nuuk."

Petra waited for a cue from Maratse, as the colour drained from Kista's face. Maratse slipped his notebook inside his pocket and nodded for Petra to continue.

"I don't know what you want," Kista said.

"It's what *you* want, really," Petra said. "What we need is proof that you have knowingly sold CITES protected products to tourists living outside of Greenland. From your discussion with Mr Keenly, we know *how* you do it. What we want is the name of the person acting on your behalf, and with the evidence you provide us, we will go and pick him up."

"Should I have a lawyer?" Kista asked.

"Of course," Petra said, tapping her hand against Maratse's leg.

"Or perhaps, I could talk to Mr Keenly…" he said.

"And tell him how cooperative you have been," Petra said.

Kista beckoned to her assistant, pulling her close and whispering in her ear. The three of them waited in silence as the assistant rummaged in the office and returned with a rectangular metal fire-proof box. Kista opened it with a key she kept around her neck, and then told her assistant to help the tourists at the back of the shop.

"She has nothing to do with it," Kista said, as soon as her assistant was out of earshot.

Maratse nodded as Kista opened the box.

"There are no certificates," Kista said, as she laid three pages of A4 paper onto the counter, "only a list of what was sold, and for how much."

"And no names?" Petra asked.

Kista shook her head. "Only initials." She pointed at the column on the far right. "KS is me." She ran her finger down a long list of items including a description followed by the artist's name and a sum of money in Danish kroner.

"Do the artists get paid?" Petra asked.

"No."

"But you do?"

"Yes."

"And who is QV?" Maratse asked.

Kista pressed her fingers against the surface of the counter as they started to tremble. The skin beneath her nails turned white.

"I'm cooperating," Kista said.

"You're doing really well," Petra said.

Maratse tapped his finger next to the initials. "Who is this?"

"He'll know this came from me."

Maratse tilted his head to catch Kista's eye. "Who is *he*?"

"Qaqi Valerius," she whispered. "He's…"

"Not a nice man," Petra said. "Yes. We know who he is." She reached for the papers. "I'm going to take these and make copies. You can expect to hear from us very soon."

Maratse pressed his hand lightly on Petra's, as he tapped a finger on the name of one of the artists listed in the column.

"Mikkiki," he said. "This is Nappartuku Mikkiki?"

"Yes."

"And why is there no initial by his name? No money in the column?"

"They are special orders," Kista said. "They haven't been sold yet."

"But they've been carved?" Petra asked. "They are ready to be sold?"

"Yes."

Maratse turned the third piece of paper and traced his

finger in the description column beside Tuku's name. "And here," he said. "Tuku's name is written fifteen times, but only seven have a description. Why is that?"

"The ones without a description? He hasn't made them yet," Kista said.

It was Maratse's turn to frown. "I don't understand."

"Qaqi has an agreement with Nappartuku. He has agreed to make fifteen pieces for Qaqi. I sell them when a tourist shows an interest, one of Qaqi's people delivers them and collects the money. Cash. No credit cards."

"And what happens when Nappartuku has made all fifteen pieces?" Petra asked.

"Then he can go home," Kista said.

"Do you know where he is?" Maratse asked.

"No," she said. "Only Qaqi knows that."

Maratse gathered the three sheets of paper into his hands, nodded at Petra, and walked towards the entrance.

"You'll hear from us," Petra said, as she followed Maratse out of the door. "She's scared," she said, as she joined Maratse on the street.

"And Qaqi has Tuku."

"Yes. He's not just missing…"

"*Eeqqi*," Maratse said. "He's been kidnapped."

"It sounds like it. Maybe it makes sense to have Gaba and the SRU after all." Petra pressed her hand on Maratse's arm. "What is it? You're spacing."

"Thinking," he said.

"Want to share?"

"It might be nothing, but…" Maratse paused to look at the gift shop sign. He dug into his pocket and pulled out the crumpled business card. "I don't know," he said. "It might be nothing."

"Okay, but we need to get going." Petra swiped the

screen of her smartphone to check the time. "Gaba will be ready now. We have to go. Maybe you *should* have a gun?"

"No time," Maratse said.

Petra called Gaba as they crossed the street, confirming that they had the proof they needed, but no address for Qaqi.

"We think Nappartuku is being held against his will," she added, as they crossed the police car park. She ended the call as Gaba led his team out of the station.

Gaba pointed at the police van parked beside the patrol car, waited for the three Special Response Unit officers, their faces obscured by masks and helmets, to get inside the van, before tossing the keys for the Toyota at Petra.

"We had a quick chat with Aqqaluk. There's a warehouse down by the docks. You follow us. Use the lights and sirens through the city. But then go quiet at the top of the hill above the docks. Questions?"

"Can I drive?" Maratse asked.

"No," Petra said. "You're supposed to be on sick leave."

"When you two are done," Gaba said, tapping the face of his watch. "We need to move."

Petra caught Maratse's eye and stuck her tongue out as she unlocked the patrol car and climbed behind the wheel. Maratse sat down in the passenger seat, fastened his seatbelt, and waited for Petra to start the engine.

"If you're good," she said, as she backed the patrol car out of the parking space and followed Gaba's van. "I'll let you turn the lights on."

Petra pulled out of the parking area and accelerated, just as Maratse turned on the emergency lights, grinning at the first wail of the siren.

Part 6

Maratse pressed his hands against the dashboard as Petra swerved around a bus and accelerated into the gap behind Gaba and the SRU. He grinned at Petra, but she ignored him, concentrating instead on following close behind Gaba, but not so close she would slam into the van if he had to suddenly brake. As they curved around the top of the hill and the road straightened ahead of them, Petra relaxed and added a little more speed.

"Keenly," she said, as she braked into the slow corner arcing through the city towards the docks. "Is he just a tourist?"

"*Iiji*," Maratse said.

"So, you lied."

"Not really. It was you who said he was undercover."

"But *you* said he was an Enforcement Agent."

"Maybe he is," Maratse said. "I never talked to him." He pointed at the van in front of them. "Next right."

Petra switched off the emergency lights and siren, braked into the turn, and slowed the patrol car to a dead stop behind Gaba's van. She unbuckled her seatbelt and got out of the car, checking her pistol while she waited for Maratse to join her.

"It's still a lie," Petra said, as she holstered her pistol.

Maratse shrugged. He scanned the road, noted the

shipping containers stacked on both sides, and the soft angles of the roofs of the warehouses behind them. Gaba had positioned the vehicles in the shadow of the containers. He organised his team, and then beckoned for Petra and Maratse to join them.

"I'm going to knock on the front door. Miki plus one is going to take the back. I want the two of you close, and ready to come on my command," he said, pointing at Petra's radio clipped to the lapel of her jacket. "But not until I give the word. Understood?"

"Yes," Petra said, as Maratse nodded.

"Good. Then we're on. As soon as we've cleared the warehouse, we'll bring you in. Hopefully, Qaqi is still inside and we can find your artist," he said, with a nod to Maratse.

"We'll wait here," Petra said.

Maratse watched the four SRU officers move into position. He had heard the name *Miki* before on a previous trip to Nuuk, but with their masks covering all but their eyes, and the helmets dwarfing their heads, the SRU were almost indistinguishable. Only Gaba, because of his height, stood out.

"That and the way he walks," Petra whispered.

Maratse noted Gaba's swagger, the way he held the submachine gun, and the general attitude he projected from the van to the front door of the warehouse. Petra's radio clicked as the SRU team indicated they were in position, and then Gaba banged on the door.

"Police," he shouted. "Open up."

The two SRU officers positioned at the back of the warehouse caught the first man to leave, tripping him into the rough grass outside the back door, as he tried to run away. Gaba caught the second man as he opened the front door, spinning him into his colleague's arms as he entered the warehouse. Gaba tucked the MP5 into his shoulder and locked his head in a straight line with the sights just before the stubby end of the visible barrel. He called for Petra and Maratse to make their way down the hill to the warehouse, meeting them at the door a minute later.

"He's not here, but there's plenty to see," Gaba said, guiding Petra and Maratse past the two men cuffed and facing the wall. Gaba led them into the workshop at the back. The air was thick with dust and the smell of burnt bone, a meaty marrow aroma that was almost pleasant. "Hobby drills at the tables," Gaba said, pointing with a stiff gloved finger. "Antlers and bones in boxes against the wall. Narwhal teeth locked in the cabinet, over there."

Maratse followed Gaba's direction and peered through a kink in the metal door of a long cabinet. He counted at least two long spiralled teeth.

"No finished figures or jewellery," Gaba said, "other than what they were working on at the tables when we arrived. But you should see this."

Gaba led them out of the workshop and up a short flight of metal stairs to the attic space above. He waited for Petra and Maratse to join him, before pointing out the mattresses and blankets on the floor, the kettle and electric hob on the cupboard against the wall, and the beer crates full of empty bottles.

"The beer surprises me, actually," Gaba said.

"It's a sweatshop," Petra said. She counted the mattresses. "Space for six to sleep here, but you've only got two."

"Right," Gaba said. "They said Qaqi took the others in a van to load a boat. Apparently, he's planning a trip north to Ilulissat, chasing the cruise ships."

"And Tuku?" Maratse asked.

"Unknown," Gaba said. "Sorry."

Gaba's radio clicked and Miki's voice crackled through the speaker.

"Van approaching. Looks like Qaqi driving."

"You're sure?" Gaba said, pressing the button on his radio to transmit.

"Pretty sure, boss."

"Then he's seen the police cars."

"*Naamik*, he came from opposite side. We're good."

"How many in the van?"

"Just Qaqi."

"Okay, we'll take him as he gets out." Gaba pointed at Petra and Maratse. "Stay here."

Maratse waited as Gaba clumped down the stairs. As soon as the SRU leader was at the bottom, Maratse followed, taking the stairs two at a time.

"David," Petra said, cursing when he ignored her, and then following a second later.

Maratse ran to the back of the warehouse and Petra followed.

"They're going to take him at the front," Petra said.

"*Iiji*," Maratse said. "All four of them. Which leaves no-one at the back."

"You're not armed."

"I've got you," he said, as he reached the back door and opened it.

Maratse ran up the hill with Petra close behind him. He stopped by the side of the patrol car and shouted for Petra to throw him the keys.

"No way. You're still on sick leave," she said, as she unlocked the car. She jabbed her fingers at the passenger seat, and then climbed in behind the wheel.

Maratse opened the passenger door, pausing at the sound of tires squealing at the bottom of the hill, before jumping into the passenger seat. "Go," he said, slapping his hand on the dashboard. Petra started the engine, shoved the Toyota into first gear and pulled out into the road.

She caught the side of Qaqi's van as he accelerated up the hill, bumping it onto two wheels and forcing Qaqi into the side of the road. The van slammed into the side of a container, shuddering to a stop. Maratse pointed as Qaqi climbed over the handbrake and onto the passenger seat. Qaqi reached for the door handle, and then leaped back as Petra slammed the Toyota into the passenger side of the van, stalling the Toyota's engine, and pinning the driver's door between the two vehicles. Maratse opened the passenger door and leaped out of the patrol car, running around the front as Qaqi kicked at the van's windscreen, smashing the glass so that he could crawl out over the bonnet. Maratse grabbed him as he slid onto the tarmac.

"Hold him," Gaba shouted, as the SRU team pounded up the road towards them.

Qaqi kicked at Maratse's leg, dropping him to the ground. Maratse rolled away from him as Qaqi scrambled to his feet and aimed a kick at Maratse's head. Maratse caught the blow on his elbows, as he twisted onto his knees. Qaqi staggered back out of Maratse's reach, then slipped his hand behind his back and tugged something long and sharp from his belt.

"Drop it," Petra said, as she raised her pistol. She spread her feet into a shooting stance, shifted her hands into a more comfortable grip around the pistol and waited for Qaqi to comply.

"Why should I?"

"Because I say so," Petra said, cutting him off as Qaqi glared at her. She nodded for Maratse to step to one side as he stood up. Then smiled as she heard Gaba and his team slow to a stop beside her. "You took your time," she said.

"And you failed to listen," Gaba said.

"Lucky for you that we did."

"Right."

Gaba and the SRU team approached Qaqi. One man removed the knife from his hand, as Gaba took his arms and cuffed him. Petra holstered her pistol and then leaned against the bonnet of the Toyota, while Gaba helped Qaqi sit on the ground.

"Maratse," Gaba said. "Ask your questions."

Maratse brushed sand and grit from his knees and then crouched in front of Qaqi. He studied him for a moment, noted the lighter ring of skin around Qaqi's neck and wondered if he had tried to commit suicide once. Qaqi's eyes blazed out of his gaunt face, glaring at Maratse.

"Nappartuku Mikkiki," Maratse said.

"What about him?"

"You know him?"

"You've seen the workshop. You know I do."

Maratse nodded. "And you made a deal with him."

"So? What if I did?"

"His granddaughter is concerned. She wants to know where he is."

"Hah," Qaqi said. He looked at Gaba, then spat to one side. "I'll bet she is. Stupid bitch."

"Hey," Gaba said. He kicked the sole of Qaqi's

shoes. "Just answer the Constable's questions."

"That's police brutality."

"Oh, you have no idea," Gaba said. "Just give me a reason."

"Later," Maratse said. He leaned closer to Qaqi. "Where is Tuku now?"

"How should I know? Our agreement is over. He's going home. Have you checked his hotel?"

"What do you mean the *agreement is over*?"

"He agreed to make fifteen pieces. He's finished," Qaqi said, lifting his chin and jutting it towards the warehouse. "There's a locker in the workshop. It's all in there."

"Show me," Maratse said.

Gaba nodded and two of his men helped Qaqi to his feet. They walked him down the hill to the warehouse, through the back door and into the workshop.

"The key's in my pocket," Qaqi said, when they stopped beside the locker.

"Careful," Gaba said, as Maratse pressed his fingers into Qaqi's pocket and removed the key.

Maratse opened the right-hand door of the cabinet, and then reached inside to flick the bolt down to open the second door; the doors squealed as he opened them wide. Apart from the two narwhal teeth, the cabinet was empty, with nothing but dust on the top shelf.

"They've stolen them," Qaqi said. "Thieves. They've taken them."

"Who's taken what?" Maratse asked.

"Tuku's Tupilaq. All fifteen of them, and a big piece that was down there," Qaqi said, stabbing his toe towards the bottom of the locker.

"Who?" Gaba said.

CHRISTOFFER PETERSEN

"That little rat, Aqqaluk. I bet it was him who told you where to find me." Qaqi laughed. "That's just perfect. The scheming little bastard." Qaqi spat at the locker.

Gaba tapped his fingers into Qaqi's chest. "Aqqaluk did this? He stole them?"

"Who else?"

"So, he had a key?"

"Obviously," Qaqi said.

"Maratse," Gaba said, beckoning him closer. "This doesn't add up. Aqqaluk's not the smartest tool in the box."

"I agree."

"Then we're missing something," Petra said.

"Oh, you have no idea," Qaqi said. He laughed again.

"What's so funny?" Gaba said, stepping in front of Qaqi. "Are you going to tell us?"

"Sure, I'll tell you. Just as soon as you let me go."

"Right, that's not going to happen."

"Fine," Qaqi said. "Then you'll never find Tuku. It'll be too late."

"Explain," Gaba said.

"You say Aqqaluk isn't smart enough for this. You're right. But he's smart enough to do what people tell him to do. Now, if someone told him that Tuku's art would be worth more if the old man was dead, what do you think he would do?" Qaqi laughed again. "He's already taken the goods, and the old man is missing. And if he dies, right after getting an award? That makes his art worth a lot more than I was ever going to make from it. But what do I know?"

"What *do* you know?" Petra said, pushing past Gaba to stand closer to Qaqi.

Qaqi pressed his face towards Petra, pushing against Gaba's hand pressed to his chest. "Would you really have shot me, Constable?"

"Yes," Petra said.

"Well, then maybe Tuku's got a chance, if he's not dead already." Qaqi twisted to look at Maratse. "Find Aqqaluk and you'll find the old man, and maybe more besides."

Part 7

The police cordon of Blok 23B was as discrete as it could be in a city of just 15,000 people, which meant that everybody knew something was going on. Children and teenagers gathered around the police cars parked at both ends of the street, creating a natural barrier of bodies, parting as Gaba and Petra drove between them and parked at the northern end of *Samuel Kleinschmidt Aqqutaa*. Petra's patrol car limped to a stop beside Gaba's van. She turned the engine off and peered up at the apartment block as Maratse removed his utility belt.

"What are you doing?"

"I don't need it," he said.

"David, this is a hostage situation."

"We don't know that for sure," Maratse said. "And if it is, a gun won't help."

"Then let Gaba go."

"Gaba doesn't speak East Greenlandic."

"Neither does Aqqaluk."

"Good," Maratse said. "Then he won't disturb us."

Maratse got out of the car. He walked as far as Gaba's van before Petra got out of the driver's side and called for him to stop.

"What are you not telling me?" she said, as she walked towards him. She pointed at the apartment block.

"Who do you think is in the apartment?"

"I don't know for sure."

"But your best guess?"

Maratse shrugged. "Trust me, Piitalaat."

"I do *trust* you, but right now I don't understand you." Petra sighed. "Go," she said. "I'll be here when you get back."

Gaba stopped Maratse on the road next to the last police car in the cordon.

"We'll move into position the second you're inside the apartment block. There will be two men at each end of the corridor. But the apartments are not empty. You can expect people are home, and," he said, waving at the teenagers chatting on their mobiles, filming them with their smartphones, "you can expect they know you are coming."

"*Iiji.*"

"Good luck, Maratse."

Maratse shook Gaba's hand, and then nodded at Petra. He lit a cigarette, rolled it into the gap between his teeth and stuffed his hands into his jacket pockets. Maratse walked down the street towards the entrance to the apartment block. He extinguished his cigarette with a pinch of his finger and thumb and tucked it back into the packet. Maratse climbed the first set of stairs, swapping a few words with the residents, exchanging smiles, and receiving insults, as he climbed to the second floor. He walked along the corridor, imagining Gaba's men moving into position as he approached Aqqaluk's apartment. He remembered Petra's face, how frustrated she was that he wouldn't tell her what or even *who* he expected to find in the apartment. He hoped Tuku was there, but he was almost certain he would find someone else too.

He wasn't surprised, then, when Fiia Mikkiki opened the door.

"I thought they would send you," she said, lapsing into the soft consonants of East Greenlandic.

"I wanted to come," Maratse said. "Will you let me in?"

"Do I have a choice?"

"Always."

"And what happens if I let you in? Are you going to arrest me?"

"Not right now."

"What does that mean?"

Maratse leaned to one side to look around Fiia. He nodded at Aqqaluk as he fidgeted in the corridor, just a few steps behind Fiia.

"You know each other?" Maratse asked.

"He's my boyfriend," Fiia said. "We met in gymnasium, here in Nuuk."

Maratse nodded. "Can I come in, Fiia?"

Fiia opened the door and Maratse stepped inside the flat. He lifted his jacket, as Aqqaluk looked at his belt.

"No gun," he said. "I don't think I need one."

Fiia brushed past Maratse and he followed her into the living room. Aqqaluk stayed in the corridor, leaning against the bathroom door. Fiia flopped onto the couch and lit a cigarette. She offered one to Maratse.

"I don't smoke inside," he said.

"Suit yourself."

Maratse looked at the yellow walls, the television standing on a plank of wood supported on two plastic milk crates. There was a withered plant in a pot on the windowsill. It might have been a Geranium once, before the summer sun and cigarette smoke sucked the life out of it. Maratse sat on the chair opposite the couch and waited for Fiia to speak.

"You're looking for *ata*," she said.

"You said he was missing."

"He was."

"But not anymore?"

"I know where he is."

"Is he here?" Maratse asked.

"Maybe."

"Fiia," Maratse said. "A few days ago, you asked for my help. Why?"

"Do you really want to know?"

"*Iiji*. That's why I'm here."

"I don't know," she said. "Maybe I was scared of what was happening, or what I wanted to do."

"What do you want to do? Fiia?"

Fiia took a long drag on her cigarette, blowing the smoke towards the ceiling, before looking at Maratse.

"*Ata* is sick," she said. "You saw him at the exhibition. He's so thin. So tired. He has cancer."

"I'm sorry."

"It's in the pancreas. The doctors said he won't live."

"But he can be treated. Maybe he will live longer," Maratse said.

"And then I have to look after him for longer. When do I get to live my life?"

Maratse waited for Fiia to finish her cigarette. He turned to look at Aqqaluk as he moved closer to the living room. A soft knocking pulled Aqqaluk back to the bathroom door. Maratse turned back to Fiia.

"Who's in the bathroom?" he asked.

Fiia said nothing.

"Is it Tuku?"

"He's going to die anyway," she said. "They just don't know when." Fiia clenched her fists in her lap and bit her bottom lip. "They want him to go to Denmark. They said they can treat him there, and that he might live another six months." Fiia glared at Maratse. "*Six months*. That's six months of taking him to the bathroom. Six months of cleaning his dirty sheets, his underwear, and… and…"

"Fiia," Maratse said. "We can get someone to help you."

"In Ittoqqortoormiit? Right, of course you can. You can just snap your fingers and there will be nurses, and doctors, someone to make food, someone to make the bed. Just like there was when my mother died of cancer, and my father committed suicide. So much help. Is *that* the kind of help you mean? Or are you going to come and visit every time *ata* needs to take a shit?"

Maratse waited for Fiia to stop, to take a breath. He stood up, holding his hands up, palms out, for Aqqaluk, as he walked into the kitchen, found the cleanest glass, and poured Fiia a glass of water. He paused at the sight of a cardboard box on the counter, checked the contents, and examined one of Tuku's carvings. Maratse closed the box. He gave Fiia the glass of water, and then sat down.

"How old were you when your mother died?"

"Fourteen."

"And your father?"

"He hung himself a month later. *Ana*, my grandmother, died before I was born." Fiia nodded towards the bathroom. "He's all the family I have left."

"Tuku is your mother's father?"

Fiia nodded, then sipped at her water.

"Can I see him, Fiia?" Maratse asked.

He waited for her to nod, and then stood up. Maratse stepped into the corridor, waited for Aqqaluk to step to one side, and then knocked on the bathroom door. The door was unlocked. Maratse opened it, then pressed his hand over his mouth, trapping his nose behind his fingers until he felt confident he could breathe without gagging.

"Tuku," Maratse said, as he knelt beside the old man. "Are you all right?"

Maratse pressed the door against the bathtub as he untied the rope around Tuku's wrists, tugged a dirty towel over his legs to hide his soiled trousers, before pressing his hand to Tuku's cheek, raising his head to look into his eyes.

"He's sick," Aqqaluk said.

"*Iiji.*"

"He needs a doctor, but Fiia said no."

"Then maybe you can go get one," Maratse whispered. He nodded at the door. "Hold your hands above your head on your way out. Don't run. There are police officers in the corridor. They will help you." Maratse looked Aqqaluk in the eye. "Do you understand, Aqqa?"

"*Aap.*"

"Then go, quietly. I will look after Fiia."

Fiia shouted for Aqqaluk as he stepped out of the apartment. Maratse stood up and walked into the corridor, as Fiia got up from the couch.

"It's all right," he said. "He's gone to get help."

Fiia flicked her gaze towards the bathroom, and then darted into the kitchen. Maratse heard the rattle of cutlery as she opened a drawer. Fiia grabbed a knife, thrusting it towards Maratse as he walked into the kitchen. She threatened him until he backed away towards the wall.

"I'll use it," she said.

"I believe you."

The knife wobbled in Fiia's hand. Maratse looked at it. Fiia saw where he was looking and then pressed the tip of the knife to her neck.

"I should have done this a long time ago," she said, as the first drop of blood dribbled onto the blade.

"Fiia," Maratse said, raising his hands. He held his palms up as he took a tiny step towards her.

"But I thought maybe something good could come of it all. *Ata* is famous. People buy his work, but he gets so little for it. I met Aqqaluk in Nuuk. He told me about Qaqi, and what he got when he sold Tupilaq to the tourists. Stupid tourists," Fiia said, and spat. She pressed the knife a little harder as Maratse took another step towards her. "They love those ugly figures; they think they're so cute. And *ata* makes them – the uglier the better. Then he gets an award and they're flying him to Nuuk for a prize. That's when I knew I could make some money. Get something for all the shit I've had to do…"

"Fiia," Maratse said. "I understand. Let me help you."

"How can you understand? Are your parents dead?"

"*Iiji.*"

"They are?"

"My father died in a helicopter accident," Maratse said.

"And your mother?"

"Suicide," he said.

"How old were you?"

"Seven." Maratse lowered his hands. "I was angry, too. It's not fair. I know, Fiia. I know it's not fair."

"He's in pain."

"*Iiji.*"

"But I couldn't kill him. That's why I came to you."

"I know."

"You were supposed to stop me."

"I'm here to help you, Fiia," Maratse said.

Fiia ignored him. Her knuckles turned white as she gripped the knife. "But if you ask him, that's what he wants. You ask him," she said, waving the knife towards the bathroom. "Ask him," she screamed.

Maratse lunged for Fiia's arm, wrapping his arm around it, trapping it against his ribs. She twisted her hand, slicing the knife against his jacket, as he curled his leg around the back of hers and swept her legs out from under her. Maratse grabbed Fiia's free arm and lowered her onto the kitchen floor, turning his head to one side as she spat at his face, and tried to bite him.

"It's okay," he said. "It's okay."

"You shit," she screamed. "Let me go, you shit."

Maratse felt the knife cut into his jacket as Fiia stabbed it into his side. He felt the point pierce his skin, and he grunted, biting away the pain, as he pressed his body on top of hers, pinning her to the floor.

"It's okay," he said, as Fiia's screams softened into sobs.

Maratse breathed as the knife slipped out of his side. He heard it clatter on the floor as Fiia let go of it.

"It's okay," he said. "Let me help you."

"I don't want your help," Fiia whispered, choking on another sob. She twisted her head at the sound of boots clumping along the corridor, and voices inside the apartment. "I don't want anyone's help."

"I know," Maratse said, as Petra entered the kitchen. "But I'm going to help you anyway."

He nodded at Petra as she knelt beside him. She pushed the knife to one side.

"Tuku?" Maratse whispered.

"With the medics," Petra said. She reached out to inspect the tear in Maratse's jacket. "You're bleeding."

"Only a little." Maratse took a breath. "Help me with her," he said.

Petra nodded, and together they helped Fiia into a sitting position. Petra pulled a small first aid kit from her belt and cleaned the knife wound on Fiia's neck.

"Is he your friend?" Fiia asked Petra in Danish.

"Yes," she said.

"You're lucky."

"We both are," Petra said. "Because I heard him promise to help you."

Fiia looked at Maratse. "Will he?"

"Yes," Petra said. "He helps everybody. That's his weakness."

The End

Author's Note

I confess, *Scrimshaw* is an indulgence. I have shoehorned all my favourite characters into this novella. Some have cameos, others are just mentioned, whilst the three main characters of Petra, Gaba and, of course, Maratse, take centre stage. It has occurred to me that people jumping into the later novellas might not know these people, and certainly not as well as I do. If that is the case, then I can only hope that the story was sufficiently entertaining to encourage you to try the first novella, *Katabatic*.

In *Scrimshaw* I have explored some of the underlying tensions that can be found in Maratse's first novel: *Seven Graves, One Winter*. The novellas are set before the novels, but I have been deliberately ambiguous with the dates, in order to let me play in Maratse's Greenland for an unlimited space of time.

Again, your patience is appreciated.

Scrimshaw brings a number of Greenlandic issues into the limelight, not least the question of souvenirs carved from whale and walrus bones. The CITES agreement exists to protect endangered flora and fauna, and it is my hope that tourists to Greenland will respect and support the work of local artists, and refrain from buying souvenirs that cannot be taken out of the country. I do realise that it can, sometimes, be difficult to do both.

Chris
August 2019
Denmark

Asiaq

~ A short story of endurance and adversity in the Arctic ~

In Greenlandic mythology
Asiaq is the goddess of the weather
she lives out on the pack ice

Part 1

I write people stories, not *Titanic* stories. That's what I told my editor, to which he replied, "The Titanic was full of people." There was nothing more I could say. He had made his point and all further discussion was little more than hot air that I expended, and he ignored. Seventy-two hours later, and I was huddled with a group of twenty-one journalists at the tiny Danish military outpost called *Station Mestersvig*, tucked inside the bottom right-hand corner of the North East Greenland National Park, on a peninsular north of Ittoqqortoormiit, and more or less on the same line of latitude as the Norwegian island of Jan Mayen. I had never been this far north before. I felt like I was being punished.

I wasn't the only one.

Constable David Maratse stood to one side of the journalists, his hands tucked into his jacket pockets as he stared beyond the shadow of the runway control tower towards the sea. I could just imagine him wishing he was in a smaller boat, checking his longline for halibut, or maybe even hunting a rogue polar bear that had been bothering the residents of a settlement further down the coast. Cruise ships, like the one-hundred-and-fourteen-metre bright red and black-hulled pride of *Arctic Horizon*'s fleet anchored just off the coast, would not interest him. Although its heritage might. *MS Gjøa* traced its lineage all the way back to Roald Amundsen's wooden sloop of the same name, the first vessel to sail through the Northwest Passage back in 1906. Maratse would undoubtedly prefer to be aboard the smaller historic vessel than its massive cousin, but *massive* was why we were gathered in Mestersvig on the first day of SAREX, the international Search and Rescue Exercise comprising elements and assets from the Canadian and Danish military, the Icelandic Coast Guard, and the *Gjøa* playing the role of the stricken cruise ship in need of rescue. The journalists had been invited to cover the exercise, while first year cadets from Greenland's Police Academy would play the role of the victims lost overboard.

"They will be wearing survival suits," Constable Petra Jensen said, explaining the cadet's role, and pointing out the important difference between the cadets in the exercise and tourists lost at sea. She paused as the journalists asked how many cadets would be taking part, and how they would be rescued. "Nine cadets in all," she said. "And they will be rescued by Canadian medics trying out a new method of parachuting into the sea, providing care and stabilising the victims while other assets race to the area."

"Parachuting into the Greenland Sea?" I asked, catching Maratse's eye.

"Yes," Petra said. "I think it's best if Løjtnant Karl Bloch from the Danish Navy's Communications Office answers specific questions. I can only speak for the cadets."

"One more question – Jessica Polley, from *The Times* – is that why you're here, Constable? To look after the cadets?"

"The Commissioner asked me to tag along," Petra said. "So, I suppose the answer is *yes*. Although, I'm not attached to the Police Academy. Unfortunately, their representative is ill. I'm the replacement."

"And your colleague?" Polley asked. "Constable?"

"David Maratse," Petra said. Maratse flicked his gaze from the sea to the journalists in front of him. "He's not from the Academy either." Petra paused, and I noticed an indulgent smile crease her cheeks. "He's being punished."

Maratse stiffened at a wave of soft laughter from the journalists and the Navy liaison officer.

"Punished? Can you clarify?"

I was confident that I knew the answer, already, but looked forward to Petra's response while enjoying Maratse's sudden twinge of discomfort.

"I'm not sure it's relevant," Petra said.

"Just a bit of background," Polley said. "For the human angle. Perhaps Constable Maratse might tell us?"

Maratse shrugged. "The Commissioner wanted to send two officers with the cadets."

"For support?"

"*Iiji*," he said.

"I'm sorry? What was that?"

The Danish Løjtnant took a step forward. "Perhaps, to provide a little clarification," he said, with a nod to Maratse, "it's important to remember that Search and Rescue in Greenland is a multidisciplinary operation, coordinated by Joint Arctic Command in the Greenland capital of Nuuk. Constable Maratse is based in Ittoqqortoormiit, just south of here. East Greenland receives thousands of tourists each summer, the majority of whom arrive in cruise ships, like *Gjøa*," he said, pointing at the cruise ship. "It's quite likely that, in the event of a disaster, local resources such as Constable Maratse, may be the first to raise the alarm. They might even be first on the scene."

"Ah, if I might follow up on that," a tall journalist said, as he pushed forwards to the front of the group.

"And your name is?"

"Marc Tilly, with *The Post*," Tilly said, rolling his broad shoulders as he pressed record on his digital recorder. "You say that *local resources* might be the first on scene, but what can one Constable do when faced with a sinking ship with a couple hundred tourists?"

"That's a good question," Bloch said. "Of course, Constable Maratse would be just one part of the SAR operation. His role would likely involve liaising with the hospital in Ittoqqortoormiit, in preparation to receive survivors."

"Ah, yeah, that's great," Tilly said, "but as I understand it, the hospital in Ittoqqortoormiit is more of a medical centre, and the population of the settlement would fit inside the *Gjøa*. What then?"

Tilly held the digital recorder towards Bloch as the journalists around him nodded, scratching notes on their jotters, or shielding their tablets from the sun as they typed the response directly into a document. Maratse took a step closer to Petra, whispering something in her ear as the Løjtnant tackled Tilly's question.

"You're right. We would probably fly straight to Tasiilaq…"

"With just a couple thousand inhabitants," Tilly said. "With just one cruise ship, you're adding a quarter of the population, stretching the resources of hospitals that are not equipped for these kinds of emergencies, on this scale."

"Of course…"

"And," Tilly said, pressing his point. "I believe I'm correct in saying that not only are the resources limited, but so are the drugs. I heard that most of the small hospitals only have a couple of shots of adrenaline, for example, to deal with heart failure, mostly because heart failure is not a common disease among the elderly in Greenland. How is a remote hospital in Greenland going to accommodate five hundred survivors, most of whom are over sixty, with more than two potential cases of heart failure, maybe more if they've been exposed to the sea, and are suffering from hypothermia?"

Bloch took a breath, nodding a couple of times as the journalists waited for his response. The question had certainly piqued everyone's interest, including Maratse's, and I wondered how often he might have considered the same scenario? Petra tugged on Maratse's jacket and whispered something as he bent his head. He nodded, and she took a step forwards, standing slightly in front of Bloch, shielding him from the journalists.

"These are good questions, and they are most relevant. We'll do our best to answer all your questions during the exercise. Constable Maratse and I will be with you, together with Løjtnant Bloch, onboard *Gjøa*. I'd like to suggest that we wrap up here and get onboard. The crew and staff from *Arctic Horizons* will show you to your cabins, and then we'll brief you on the next stages of the exercise."

Tilly raised his hand.

"Yes?" Petra said.

"I have a quick follow-up."

"One follow-up, and then we really must get onboard."

"It's about the weather," Tilly said, gesturing at the thick grey clouds competing with the sun above them. "The forecast doesn't look good – strong winds, and maybe even a snowstorm, which is strange…"

"It's Greenland," Bloch said.

"Yes," Tilly said. "It's also June." He looked at Petra. "I just want to know if the exercise is going to go ahead?"

"That's the one thing we'll never be able to control," Petra said. "If we can't operate in a snowstorm, what use are we?"

"And the cadets?" Polley asked. "You're responsible for them. When do you decide it's too dangerous for them to be in the water? *We're* going to be on a ship – at least, I hope so." Polley smiled as the journalists around her laughed.

"Commander Dohm on the HDMS *Knud Rasmussen*, has the overall command at the local level," Petra said. "He'll make that decision, if necessary." Petra waited for the journalists to settle, and then pointed at the motorboats moored just off the beach below the station. "Now, if you'll follow Jóhanna Guðmundsdóttir, she'll take you down to the boats."

Jóhanna, a slim Icelander of medium height wearing the classic wool sweater beneath a thin *Arctic Horizon* company jacket, breezed past Maratse, her blonde hair drifting across her face in the light wind blowing from the sea. I waited as my journalist colleagues zipped their jackets, clicked the plastic buckles on their satchels and photo bags, and tugged at the Velcro fasteners around their cuffs. We wore the same light blue windproof jacket as Jóhanna, courtesy of *Arctic Horizon*, good quality, but not quite as warm as the police jackets worn by Petra and Maratse. Jóhanna helped us into the slim lifejackets we were required to wear on the journey to *Gjøa*. She helped us close the buckles and advised us not to pull the tag that fired the CO2 cartridge.

"Because then you'll just blow-up," she said, in her charmingly accented English.

We laughed, adjusted the straps as per Jóhanna's directions, and then walked with her down to the beach. Maratse and Petra grabbed a lifejacket and followed us, while Bloch said something about joining us later.

The sea, in contrast to the sand and grit stretched between black-lichened boulders and pale green Arctic grasses, was a rich blue, inviting but punishingly cold, as Tilly reminded me as we waited on the beach for our turn to board the motorboat.

"Without a survival suit," he said, "we're talking a few minutes, tops. Even with a suit, your hands will cramp with the cold and you won't be able to use your fingers – you can't grab or hold anything in these temperatures without protection." He fingered the emergency tag on the lifejacket. "Without insulation, these things are just going to keep you afloat, so they can take your body home."

"You've done your research," I said.

"Sure," he said. "This whole thing is just a *Titanic* waiting to happen. The Danish Navy Commanders have been talking about it for years. But they haven't got the resources to chaperone a cruise ship up and down the coast. There was talk of making it a requirement for at least two cruise ships to sail together, but the travel companies don't like that. They sell high-end exclusive adventure cruises. Who's going to pay good money for an exclusive trip, when every photo you take has another cruise ship in the background?"

"You're right," I said.

"Yeah, probably, but, tell me something else." Tilly nodded towards Maratse and Petra standing a few metres further up the beach. "I saw you nod at the Constable there. Do you know him?"

"Yes," I said. "We've had some experiences together."

"*Experiences*? Have I read about them?"

"You might have, if you read Danish?"

"No," Tilly said. "But tell me this, why is he here, I mean really? It's clear that he's not being punished. Look at this boat," he said, pointing at *Gjøa*. "I've seen the menu, and photos of the cabins. I don't mind admitting that, even though the terrain isn't exactly inspiring, when my editor wanted a volunteer to spend three days on a cruise ship in the Arctic, they had to beat me back with a stick. That's hardly what I call a punishment assignment."

"Well," I said. "I agree with you there. But you don't know Maratse."

I could have continued, adding more background and even sharing some of the adventures we had had together, but the look on Maratse's face said it all – three days on a luxury cruise ship surrounded by journalists wasn't just punishment, it was torture.

Part 2

_____

The *MS Gjøa* was an impressive ship. The hull was painted black from the sharp tip of the bow, stretching all the way to the forward-facing racy angle of the stern. The rest of the ship shone like a beacon in letter-box red, save for the white stripes circling the exhaust stacks. It reminded me of the Russian nuclear icebreakers chartered by the more adventurous cruise ship companies. However, though not quite an icebreaker, *Gjøa* still had an ice class rating of 1B.

"Which means she can forge ahead through brash and pancake ice, but really shouldn't try anything too exciting," Tilly said, as we climbed the stairs zigzagging up the starboard side of the ship.

Jóhanna gathered us by the door of the sixth deck, explaining that there were eight decks in all, and that she would be guiding us through the entire ship just as soon as we were settled in. She led us up a flight of stairs to the restaurant on deck five, where the galley staff showed us to a table of refreshments. Maratse and Petra stood to one side as we made ourselves comfortable. I caught Maratse's wistful gaze out of the window, and the soft snap of Petra's fingers as she slapped his leg and whispered something out of the side of her mouth. I couldn't hear what she said, but the word *focus* came to mind.

"Before the tour of the ship," Jóhanna said, "I'd like to introduce you to Seth McCormack."

She smiled as a rugged man with a full beard strode across the deck to join her. The beard, I noticed, concealed a hair lip, not that he seemed to be bothered by it. There was little about Seth McCormack that suggested he was easily fazed or insulted. Despite Tilly's sharp-edged questions, I felt far more optimistic about participating in an Arctic Search and Rescue exercise than I had when my editor first suggested it. People like Seth, well… it's hard not to feel confident. I cast another glance at Maratse. In appearance, at least, the two men could not be more different, and I wondered if Seth McCormack could walk the walk as well as he did the talk.

"Thanks, Jóhanna, and welcome," Seth said, as he turned on the charm. "We're rather proud of our flagship, and excited to be a part of an important exercise."

"But aren't you losing money?" Polley asked. "Or are you being paid to participate."

"No, not at all," Seth said. "We're not getting paid to be a part of SAREX. Usually a naval ship will play the part of the stricken cruise ship in exercises like these. But when we discussed the possibility of our company, *Arctic Horizon*, taking part, then it made sense to all parties. This is what it's all about. Why shouldn't we take a week out of our schedule to participate? If I had to guess," he said, turning his deep blue eyes on each of us as he scanned the group, "the name *Titanic* has cropped up more than once in your notes. There's twenty-one of you here. I'm guessing that's at least twenty references to that famous ship." He pointed to the panoramic windows on either side of the restaurant. "There's not many icebergs in this stretch of water today, but with today's technology, and the superior design of *Gjøa*, while it might be tempting to draw reference to *The Titanic*, it would not be accurate. I hope, during your stay with us, we can show you why. But for now, I'll leave you with Jóhanna."

Seth gave a brief dip of his head and a short but lingering smile, before exiting the restaurant, promising to return and answer more questions at dinner. I watched him leave and saw him lurch by the door as a sudden gust pressed against the port side of the ship, catching him unawares. Maratse checked his balance with a slight shuffle, nodding at Petra as she gripped the back of a chair to steady herself. Jóhanna tried to laugh it off, but I wondered if the sudden gust was a premonition, if we hadn't already jinxed the exercise more than once with the name *Titanic*?

"Refreshments," Jóhanna said. "Tea, coffee and soda, before we begin the tour."

The sound of the ship's engines rumbled through the deck as the Captain compensated for another gust against the bow. *Gjøa* turned into the wind, and I saw two more ships loitering further out to sea. White caps broke against their bows as they maintained just enough forward momentum to hold position. The HDMS *Knud Rasmussen* was easy to identify, having spent a little time onboard, but the grey ship with the red, white and blue stripes of the Icelandic flag painted on its side was new to me.

"That's the Icelandic Coast Guard," Maratse said, as he joined our table. He reached over the back of a chair and poured a cup of coffee. "It's called *Óðinn*," he said.

"You mean *Odin*?"

Maratse raised his eyebrows, then took two lumps of sugar from the bowl beside the coffee, dipping each one into his cup and then sucking the coffee out of it. Petra nudged him to one side and poured a cup of tea.

"It's a new ship," Maratse said. "They've still got teething troubles."

"What kind of trouble?" Tilly asked, as he turned around. He looked at Maratse and waited for a response.

"Engine trouble," he said, before adding, "Maybe," when Petra tapped his arm.

Tilly let it go and turned his attention to Petra. "Where are the cadets? Aren't you supposed to be looking after them?"

"They're onboard *Knud Rasmussen*. The Commander will put them into the water once the exercise starts.

"About that," Tilly said. "Are you allowing for the fog of war?"

"What?"

"The unknown," he said. "It all seems rather well orchestrated. Makes it difficult to imagine how the different agencies would act in a real emergency." Petra started to speak, but Tilly cut her off with a question for Maratse. "How about you, Constable? How would you react when you got the call that a cruise ship hit an iceberg off Scoresbysund?"

"Ittoqqortoormiit," Maratse said.

"Same place, same question," Tilly said, reaching for a bottle of coke.

Maratse glanced at me before sipping his coffee. I might have pestered him in the past, begging to come with him for the sake of a story, or even ignoring orders and my own safety to join Maratse on a search or help him with an investigation, but we had an understanding. I would never bother him with questions, not like Tilly. Sure, I might ask questions, but usually when I didn't understand something, not because I was trying to put him on the spot or catch him unawares. Fortunately for Maratse, Petra had spent a lot more time around Tilly's breed of journalist than he had. She sat down next to him and started to explain the procedures Løjtnant Bloch had touched on earlier. Maratse slipped away towards the door and I followed him.

The *Gjøa*'s Captain interrupted the light chatter around the refreshments table with an announcement over the ship speakers that the next twenty minutes might be a little bumpy, as they pushed through the waves to join the other ships just beyond the peninsula.

"It's best if you remain seated for the time being," he said, before apologising for the inconvenience.

Maratse and I sat down at the table closest to the door. The bow lifted with each wave, and then the ship dropped into the trough. Waves rebounding off the coast created a choppy quartet of force that lifted the ship on one side and then the other. The first journalists started to pale. Maratse sipped his coffee.

"I didn't expect to see you so soon," I said, preferring to talk than to think about my stomach, and the effect the *Gjøa*'s roll and pitch had on it. "Are you really being punished?"

"Petra said I had to come," Maratse said. "I was supposed to be on leave. She said it would be like a holiday."

"On a cruise ship?"

"*Iiji*," he said. "But maybe not so rough."

I gripped the edge of the table, turning my head at the clatter of cups and saucers sliding off the table and smashing on the deck. Maratse lifted his head at a string of shocked exclamations and curses rippling through the journalists' ranks.

"They probably wish they were still on shore," I said.

"And you?"

"Yes. I wish I was there, too."

"You'll be all right," Maratse said. "Find a fixed point on the horizon and stare at it."

He stood up as the radio clipped to the lapel of his jacket crackled into life. Maratse responded and then stepped to one side, nodding and waving for Petra to join him.

"That doesn't look good," Tilly said, as he staggered across the deck to sit next to me. "Petra was just telling me about the response times. It's impressive given the sheer size of the country, but then they've never been tested on a large scale before."

"That's interesting," I said, as I pressed my hand to my mouth. I took a few deep breaths and then looked at Tilly. "You don't get seasick?"

"Nope," he said. "It has to be really bad."

"This isn't?"

"Not yet." Tilly pressed his hand on my arm and nodded at Petra and Maratse huddled in close conversation. "Something's not right," he said. "Look at them. Whispers and bad luck, I'll bet you. With any luck, we might get a real story out of this one."

"The exercise is not enough?"

"Sure," Tilly said. "Maybe for page thirteen in a broadsheet or buried in a weekend travel supplement. But if something actually happens to spice it up a bit. This could turn out to be very worthwhile indeed."

I didn't need more to happen, and neither did my colleagues. When the first man and woman threw up, I was keen to join them, but the look on Petra's face gave me some measure of control. It seemed there were worse things than seasickness going on. I looked out of the panoramic window on the port side, searching for something to focus on, something solid on the horizon. But the seas were building with grey waves turning black beneath stormy skies.

"This is it," Tilly said, slapping my arm as the ship's speakers hissed with an open channel to the Captain.

"Sorry, folks, this is going to take a little longer than ten minutes. We're going to push through to calmer seas. Everything should settle once we get a little further from the coast." The Captain's words were punctuated by a second crash of crockery. "Nothing to be worried about. Nothing this boat can't handle. The crew will take care of you."

I looked around the restaurant, recognising the crew by their uniforms, not their faces – they were as pale as ours. Jóhanna's rosy cheeks that had complemented her Icelandic complexion so well back on shore, were grey now, grey beneath long blonde hair that clung to her skin with nauseous beads of sweat.

A blast of cold Greenlandic air gave me a sudden lift, as Maratse opened the doors at the rear of the restaurant and helped Petra onto the balcony. The door banged shut behind them, but that moment of reprieve was enough to give me the energy to stagger past the tables and over the chairs to the balcony. I opened the door, bracing myself in the wind, and gagging at the sound of Petra vomiting over the side. They stood on the port side of the ship. Maratse held Petra's hair from her face as he shouted into the radio – something Greenlandic, something urgent.

"What's going on?" I asked, as I gripped the railing to the right of Maratse and Petra.

Maratse nodded into the wind. The first thick flakes of snow caught in his hair and melted against my cheek, as I stared in the direction Maratse had nodded. *Odin*, the Icelandic Coast Guard cutter with the country's colours blazed across its hull, was listing to port, turning with the waves. The emergency navigation lights were lit, but the windows on the bridge were dark.

Maratse leaned into the wind. "No power," he shouted. "No control."

I checked our course, felt the laboured rumbling of *Gjøa*'s engines through the deck, and realised that the Captain was struggling to keep an even keel in the teeth of a sudden Arctic storm. The same waves that *Gjøa* crashed up and over, were also pushing against the starboard side of the stricken Coast Guard cutter, *Odin*, and pushing it straight into our path.

Part 3

I remember watching a Steven Spielberg film when I was a teenager. I don't remember the name, but it had something to do with a big rig truck and a man in a car. The audience never saw the driver of the truck, only the huge grille filling the car's rear-view mirror, or the massive tyres seen in the side mirrors. I remember the car driver's eyes, almost bursting with fear. But what I remember most, was that the truck was behind the car. Sure, it was chasing him, relentlessly, but it was *behind* the car. The driver saw it in mirrors – *behind* him.

I truly wished the Icelandic Coast Guard cutter *Odin* was behind us. I would have given anything to be *chased*, relentlessly or not, it didn't matter. What mattered was the fact that about four thousand tonnes of uncontrollable iron and steel was bearing down on us, haphazardly, but with nature on its side, charting a course straight for us. The car driver in Spielberg's film spent a good deal of screen time wondering what the driver of the rig looked like. I couldn't see the Commander of the *Odin*, but I didn't need to see his face to know how he must have felt.

"Brace, brace for impact."

The Captain's voice preceded *Gjøa*'s alarm by a few seconds. The seven short blasts started at the same time as the Captain coaxed more power from the engines. I felt the extra power thunder through the deck, as Maratse dragged Petra from the railing with one arm curled around her waist. He grabbed my jacket collar on the way past, hauling me into the restaurant as he shouted at the journalists and crew clustered around the tables.

"Lifejackets, now."

I spun towards a chair as Maratse let go of me. He set Petra on her feet, spared a second to press his hands to her shoulders, holding her as he studied her face.

"I'm okay," she said.

Maratse nodded, let go of Petra, and then thrust a lifejacket into my chest.

"Put it on," he said. "Help them."

I turned to run to help my colleagues, only to jerk backwards as Maratse grabbed me by the shoulder.

"Put *your* lifejacket on first. *Then* help them." He paused as the eighth and longest alarm tone began to ring through the ship's loudspeakers. He shook his head, tightened the straps on my lifejacket, then propelled me towards the table of journalists as he tugged a lifejacket over his shoulders, pulled the straps beneath his legs, and buckled it at the front.

Petra lurched past me as I stumbled into the table. She grabbed Jóhanna by the sleeve of her jacket, just as the ship lurched to starboard. Petra tumbled with Jóhanna onto the deck, bumping into the steps leading up to the raised portion of the restaurant.

"Where's the rally point for the lifeboats," Petra said, as she scrambled to her feet.

"Deck four."

"And the fastest route?"

"The stairs," Jóhanna said, as Petra helped her up.

Petra pointed at the journalists, and said, "Take them with you. There are twenty-one in all. Remember that."

"Yes," Jóhanna said. She brushed her hair out of her face and called out for everyone to follow her.

"What about him?" Polley said, pointing at the crumpled form of a man lying beneath the table closest to the door. I recognised Tilly's jacket, but the blood in his hair was new.

"Help me," Maratse said, waving me over as he reached for the chairs and pulled them away from Tilly's body. "He must have hit his head on the edge of the table." Maratse pointed at Tilly's blood soaking into the white tablecloth. "Stay with him. I'll find a stretcher."

I turned as Jóhanna called out my name, urging me to join the other journalists with rapid beats of her hand. The gesture made me think of hummingbirds, and I stifled the urge to laugh, convincing myself that it was the shock of it all. The absurdity of finding ourselves in a life-threatening situation at sea, on an exercise designed to mimic the very same thing.

Of course, the situation was still developing, and the threat to our lives increasing by the second.

"I'm staying here with Tilly," I said. "You go on."

Jóhanna hesitated until Petra pressed one hand on her shoulder and pointed at the stairs with the other. "You've got nineteen journalists, and you. That's twenty souls including you," she said, shoving Jóhanna gently but firmly towards the stairs. "Go. The crew will help you."

Souls. That's the word they use in survival situations, usual the catastrophic kind. When do people stop becoming *people*? When do we stop talking about *lives* and start using the word *souls*? I didn't know, and I'm not sure Petra did either. It could have been a slip of the tongue, or an unconscious changing of gears in her mind, but when she knelt beside me, there was nothing in her face to suggest she even knew what she had said. Jóhanna was equally unfazed, too occupied with herding a gaggle of frightened journalists up a flight of stairs to the fourth deck.

"How is he?" Petra asked. She brushed her hair behind her ear and leaned over Tilly's face, pressing her ear to his mouth and nose.

"I don't know," I said.

"He's breathing," she said. Petra slid two fingers inside Tilly's collar, searching for the pulse at his neck. "There's a pulse – a little weak."

"But he's alive," Maratse said, as he stepped over the chairs lying like beach obstacles before an invasion on the deck. He gripped the table as the ship heeled to starboard, as if the Captain was yanking on the wheel to turn as sharply as possible. Maratse found his balance, let go of the table, and opened an aluminium scoop stretcher. He worked his way to the other side of the table, sliding the open stretcher either side of Tilly's body like a lobster claw. "Help me get it under his arms," he said, as Petra and I crawled under the table, lifting Tilly's shoulders and sliding the sides of the stretcher beneath him. Maratse pushed the stretcher until Petra told him to stop. We lifted his legs, and Petra clamped the stretcher closed, just beneath Tilly's feet.

"On three," she said, once Maratse was finished strapping Tilly's head between two firm blocks of rubber-coated foam.

I waited for Petra's count, grabbed one side of the stretcher, and slid Tilly out from under the table at a nod from Petra. Maratse staggered around the table and knelt at Tilly's feet, strapping them to the stretcher as Petra and I secured his legs and upper body.

"This is not going to be easy," Petra said. "We could do with one more to lift him."

"No time," Maratse said. "I'll take the feet. You take the shoulders."

Maratse paused to look us both in the eye, before we moved into a better position to lift and then carry Tilly to the stairs.

It was, in hindsight, fortunate that the collision occurred before we lifted Tilly. He was at least already on the deck when the *Odin* punctured the *Gjøa*'s port side, with a banshee-like wrenching of metal, tipping the ship onto its starboard side and flinging the three of us across the deck against the panoramic windows. Tilly spun like a loose torpedo, pinballing from one table leg to another before coming to a stop on the banister wall leading up the short flight of stairs to the restaurant's raised deck. He lay there, his downward progress stalled, for the moment, just like the trajectory of the *Gjøa*, pinned as she was on the sharp bow of the Coast Guard cutter.

Petra was the first to move, stifling a groan as she rolled onto her side. She swore as the tab of her lifejacket caught on the back of a chair. The gas cylinder fired with an insistent hiss, inflating her lifejacket and hindering her movement.

"Piss," she said, reaching for the knife at her belt to puncture the jacket.

"Piitalaat," Maratse said, as he picked himself up. "You need that."

"Not yet," she said, nodding at Tilly as the jacket deflated and she slid her knife into the sheath on her belt.

Petra picked her way across the right-angled deck, clambering over the tables until she reached me. "You okay?"

"Yes," I said, taking her hand.

"Stay off the glass."

"Will it break?"

"It might."

A long metallic wail, together with a grating sound like glass being dragged across sand, pierced the bulkhead, turning our heads as the *Gjøa* twisted. I grabbed the closest table, and then Petra's belt, as she lost her footing.

"Thanks," she said, clawing her way onto the bulkhead that used to be beneath the windows, but now ran parallel to them, like a mountain path above a raging river below.

"We have to move," Maratse said. "Have to get Tilly."

I couldn't see the Coast Guard cutter, but I pictured it and the helpless crew doing what they could to assist the crew and passengers of the *Gjøa*. I almost laughed for the second time, as I imagined the classic saying *out of the frying pan and into the fire*, as the crew of one stricken ship tried to help the other. Fortunately, there was no fire that I was aware of. All we had to do was grab Tilly and climb out of the restaurant. But climbing *out* really meant climbing *through*, as the starboard side of the *Gjøa* pressed closer and closer to the sea below us. Soon, we really would be climbing *up* to the port side of the ship.

Maratse grabbed one chair after another, tossing them to one side as he cleared a path towards Tilly. Petra and I followed in his wake, taking each other's hands when navigating a table, pressing them against each other's backs for support. Maratse reached Tilly first. He curled his hand around the top of the stretcher, nodding for us to each take a side at Tilly's feet.

"I'll lead the way," Maratse said. "Slowly."

Staggering up the restaurant deck was like walking through a haunted house at a theme park, except the pictures on the walls and the angle of the tables screwed into the floor were not designed to disorientate you, they were truly disorientating. My fingers brushed the carpet covering the deck of the restaurant, as I reached for a table leg, something solid to hold onto as we climbed towards the exit. There were voices in the corridor ahead of us, and echoes in the stairwell. Maratse guided Tilly's stretcher around the door frame, sliding it along the bulkhead so that we could take a short break to catch our breath and calm our nerves. I did both, but so long as the metallic wail continued to fill the ship, there was nothing *calm* about my nerves, and my breathing seemed to be geared to a semi-permanent pant.

"Are you all right?" Petra asked.

"Yes," I said.

She nodded and then turned to watch Maratse as he investigated the stairwell. Maratse looked over his shoulder, caught Petra's eye, and then shook his head, just slightly and ever so slowly. Petra cursed, and Maratse crawled back to crouch beside Tilly's stretcher.

"There is debris on the stairs," he said. "We can crawl over it, but it will be difficult."

"What about the voices?" I asked.

"Crew and journalists, waiting at the top of the stairs."

"They should be going to the lifeboats," Petra said.

"*Iiji,*" Maratse said. He shrugged. "I think they are

frozen."

"Cold?" I said.

"Frozen stiff. They need some motivation."

Tilly groaned as the stretcher tipped towards the bulkhead. Maratse grabbed the side of the stretcher and braced himself as the ship listed to starboard. It felt like waves had caught the *Gjøa*is stern and were pulling her by the tail as more waves pressed the bow of the Coast Guard cutter deeper into the *Gjøa*'s side, like a hunter spearing a whale with the tip of a harpoon. But a harpoon tip was supposed to break off, embedding itself in the whale, while the hunter secured the line attached to the tip to a cleat on his boat or a loop of bone on his *qajaq*.

But there was no safety line attached to the cutter, and no hunter on the other end.

"We can't stay here," Petra said, raising her voice as she pointed at the stairwell. "We have to try."

"*Imaqa*," Maratse said. "Or we go straight up, and onto the deck. If the ship turns onto her side, we climb out and wait for rescue."

"What about them?" I asked, as whimpers of pain and terror drifted down the stairwell.

"We rescue them too," he said.

Part 4

Petra pressed her hand on Maratse's arm as he started to lift Tilly's stretcher. "No," she said. "We have to get them moving up the stairs first."

"The crew can do that," Maratse said, curling his hand around the stretcher's aluminium tubes.

"But listen to them," Petra said, pointing towards the stairwell. "They're not moving. Look at the resources we've got right here – two police officers. We need to split up and get people moving, before it's too late."

In all the time I had known Maratse, I had seen few expressions that could be easily interpreted. He had many nuances of the same unfathomable features, interspersed with a slight curling of his lip or a glitter of something dancing in his eyes, but generally speaking, he wore a kind of *catch-all* look that suggested a casual indifference. I knew it wasn't true, of course, he cared deeply about his people and his land, but it was only when he was emotionally torn that his expression changed, as it did then, when Petra told him they should split up. He had probably had the same thought, but when acting on it meant leaving Petra behind on a sinking ship – literally –then the associated turmoil creased his brow and sowed doubt in his eyes.

That's when I knew we really were in trouble.

"It makes sense to leave us here," Petra said. "We'll

slide the stretcher up the hall towards the port side of the ship. You get the journalists and the crew into the lifeboats."

"Hmm," Maratse said. He reached across Tilly and took Petra's hand, squeezed it once, before nodding at me and letting go of the stretcher. "Use the radio," Maratse said. "Stay in contact."

Maratse climbed to the stairwell, with one foot on the floor and the other on the wall, with the apex of the two beneath him. He cast one last look over his shoulder and disappeared from view.

"You take his legs," Petra said, as soon as Maratse was gone. "I'll carry at the head and lead the way."

"You're sure we shouldn't try the stairs?"

"No," she said. "It won't help. We'll spend more time trying to manoeuvre, and then we'll be stuck in the middle of the ship when she goes down." Petra caught herself, as I digested what she had just said. "Sorry," she said, when she caught the look on my face.

"It's okay."

I nodded that I was ready, and Petra began pulling the stretcher up the corridor towards the port side of the ship. I followed, trying to focus, but it was difficult. First, Petra had used the word *souls* and now she suggested it was just a matter of time before the ship sank. Perhaps her fatalism propelled her forwards. There was no time to look backwards, or to just wait in anticipation of everything working itself out, the ship righting itself and the Coast Guard cutter gently sliding along the port side towards calmer waters.

No.

She was right.

We had to keep going.

Once we passed the stairs, Petra stopped to press the transmit button on her radio.

"How are you doing, David?"

Maratse's response, just two clicks on the radio, made me smile.

"Once he gets going," I said. "You can never shut him up."

Petra bit her bottom lip, corralling a laugh behind pearly white teeth. She took a breath to compose herself before replying. "Yeah, he's a regular chatterbox," she said. She checked Tilly's pulse, held the back of her hand to his nose and mouth, and grabbed the stretcher. "David's probably busy. Let's keep going."

A stream of curses turned my head, and I stared at the entrance to the stairwell just behind us. Maratse appeared a moment later. He looked to the right, nodded at me, and then staggered along the wall until he was level with us but on the other side of the corridor.

"I need him," he said, pointing at me. "One of the women fell and broke her leg. I left her at the top of the stairs. They must have missed her in the confusion."

I'm sure he meant to say panic, but it didn't change the situation. He couldn't carry the woman by himself.

"I'll wait," Petra said. "Just go."

Maratse nodded. He peeled away from the bulkhead and half slid, half staggered back to the stairs. I swapped a look with Petra and then followed.

"Thank Christ," Polley said, as I clambered up the stairs after Maratse. "I thought he was going to leave me."

"Then you don't know, Maratse," I said, curious that I should say such a thing, but confident that it was true. I nodded that I was ready and moved to Polley's left side.

We took an arm and a leg each, carrying Polley as if she sat in a chair as we staggered along the sloping deck to the lifeboat creaking in the launch chute ahead of us.

The wind curled off the sea, spraying snow and saltwater into our faces. I caught a glimpse of the *Odin*'s bow just below the *Gjøa*'s bridge. I was struck with the image of a sperm whale, as if this was Moby Dick himself, spearing Captain Ahab's *Pequod*, holding it between massive jaws. But the *Odin*'s grip was slipping, and the previous image of the hunter returned, only this time the harpoon tip was loose. Without it there would be nothing to stop the *Gjøa* rolling onto its side in the Greenland Sea.

"Keep going," Maratse said.

He stopped at the steps up to the lifeboat hatch, pausing for a moment to apologise to Polley, before nodding to me to carry her up the steps and slide her into the lifeboat. Polley screamed as her ankle bumped against the lip of the hatch, and again when the survivors inside the lifeboat passed her from one set of hands to another, crowd-surfing the journalist into a vacant seat. Seth McCormack was there, holding his head in his hands.

"Now you," Maratse said, taking my arm.

"But Petra and Tilly?"

"I'll get them."

"Maratse," I said. "After all we've been through, do you really think I'm going to get on this lifeboat, and leave you behind?"

"I could push you inside," he said.

"But you won't."

Maratse's face softened into one of his expressions that I had seen before, the sad sagging of his eyes, followed by a brief nod of his head.

"*Qujanaq*," he said, as he stood back to close the hatch.

Maratse slapped his hand on the side of the lifeboat, then gently pushed me to one side as one of the crew launched it. It whooshed down the chute like air being sucked through a gap beneath a door only to be consumed by the fire behind it. The lifeboat was consumed by the sea, but only for a second as it bobbed back to the surface, a bright orange vessel, a transport of souls, powering towards the Danish Navy patrol vessel HDMS *Knud Rasmussen* battling the waves just a few hundred metres to the north of the Coast Guard cutter and its prey.

That's when I noticed that the sea was full of smaller vessels, lifeboats and motorboats from the *Odin*, and the *Knud Rasmussen*'s own motorboats and RHIBs. While the sea was full of activity, the air was noticeably still, and I wondered if the snowstorm had grounded the helicopters, and if the Canadian Para Rescue Jumpers were still waiting to take off from Reykjavík?

"Come on," Maratse said.

Maratse's radio crackled into life as we staggered back to the door leading inside deck four. I leaned against the bulkhead as Maratse responded to a situation report.

"Nineteen passengers plus ten crew are off the ship," he said.

"Confirm, *all* passengers."

"*Eeqqi*, negative, two passengers remaining, plus two police officers – Constable Petra Jensen and myself."

"Maratse – status of Constable Jensen?"

"She's okay."

"And the passengers?"

"One injured, possible spinal injury. Unconscious, but breathing."

"Okay, Maratse. Be advised no helicopters at this time. Maybe ten minutes. Can you get to a lifeboat?"

I looked back along the dock at the empty lifeboat chute and wondered where the others might be.

"*Imaqa*, maybe," Maratse said. He exhaled for what seemed like a whole minute before responding. "I don't know."

"Understood."

The radio crackled with what I hoped was sympathetic static, but it sounded awfully like a stutter of resignation at the hopelessness of the developing situation.

I had seen my share of rescue documentaries and marvelled at the bravery of the Coast Guard and Navy crews getting ropes around ships drifting uncontrollably towards rocky coastlines. But often it was just one ship, measurably smaller than a cruise ship, and I didn't remember seeing a rescue where two ships had collided. I *did* remember seeing crew being evacuated from oil tankers and container ships, and I wondered if that was the only option. The combined mass of the *Odin* and the *Gjøa* was probably much the same as a container ship, and I supposed the only thing they could do was evacuate. Which meant that was all *we* could do.

I turned my head as the crackle of Maratse's radio softened, and we heard the words, "Good luck, Maratse."

Maratse clicked the transmit button twice, took a long breath of stormy Greenland air, before nodding at me, and reaching for the door handle.

"Ready?"

"Yes," I said, and followed Maratse inside.

"Petra?" Maratse said, talking into his radio as we staggered back to the stairs.

"Yes."

"We're on our way back."

"I heard," she said. "At least a little. A lot of static."

"*Iiji*," Maratse said.

He let go of the radio and gestured for me to walk ahead. I took one step onto the stairs, and then missed the second as a wave slammed against the side of the *Gjøa* and wrenched it free of the *Odin*'s pointy bow. I tumbled down the stairwell, flailing after the handrail, only to slap my wrist against a metal strut securing the handrail to the wall. I'm sure I shouted a curse or two, but they were lost beneath the combined wail of the emergency alarm and the *Gjøa*'s death throe groan as it surrendered to the sea.

I fell onto the wall on the landing between decks as the stairs disappeared beneath my feet. Maratse slid down the wall and landed next to me with a thump that shuddered through my body. He turned me onto my back, reached for my wrist, pausing as I jerked it away from him.

"It's broken," I said.

Maratse started to speak but stopped at the sound of Petra sliding down the corridor floor. I turned my head as the stretcher slid into view. Tilly's feet pointed straight down towards the restaurant, and he would have gone all the way if Petra hadn't reached out to grab at a cupboard full of firefighting equipment on the way down. I could see the heels of her boots as she scraped them against the floor to arrest her fall. Maratse leaped over me and took two huge steps to the end of the bulkhead. He grabbed the stretcher, shouted to Petra that he had it, and then told her to let go and slide into the stairwell.

"I'll fall," she said.

"I'll catch you," Maratse said.

"You can't hold us both."

Maratse shifted his position, stuffing the toe of one boot inside the handhold at the top of the stretcher above Tilly's head.

"Quickly," he said, stretching his arms as Petra let go of the cupboard. She slid into view and Maratse caught her, using the momentum of her fall to sling her into the stairwell. He reached for the stretcher, gripping it as he removed his boot from the handhold.

Petra scrambled over Maratse, holding the stretcher as he changed his grip, and then, together, they pulled Tilly into the stairwell, Maratse standing, pulling up with both hands, as Petra knelt, sliding the lower half of the stretcher over the corner of the bulkhead until Tilly was flat against the bulkhead wall.

Maratse slid into a sitting position, holding his hand out for Petra, and pulling her onto the floor that used to be the stairwell wall. Neither of them said a word; they just held hands, until both their radios crackled with the latest report. Maratse turned the volume down on his own radio as Petra responded.

"Say again," she said.

"…we see smoke. The lower deck of the *Gjøa* is on fire."

Part 5

The lower deck was on fire, but was it deck eight, seven, maybe even deck six, right beneath our position? It made sense if it was the lowest deck, the one with the engine room, plenty of things to catch fire in there, especially if seawater had entered the ship and gotten into the electrical circuits. But as the *Gjøa* tipped more and more to starboard *below* was actually to our right.

"You're thinking too much," Maratse said, as he made me grip the end of his extendable baton, while wrapping a bandage from the first aid kit on his belt around it. He tied the baton like a splint to my wrist. "Okay?"

"I'm all right," I said. "I've just seen too many movies."

"Poseidon?" Petra asked. "I was thinking the same thing."

It was strange how the threat of fire seemed to be just one more thing to add to the list. We were on a stricken – probably *sinking* ship – in the Arctic, with an unconscious passenger. The world had literally turned on its side, and now there was a fire. It was perfect *Poseidon* material, and I contemplated the idea of writing *that* book, or at least its sequel, if I ever got off the ship.

"We're getting out of here," Maratse said, as if reading my mind. Given the situation, it wasn't hard, between the pain and the panic, my face creased through a range of emotions, all of which betrayed the overarching desire to get off the ship. While I would have liked to have given Maratse more credit, reading my mind in this instance was not a superpower, and if it was, then it was more or less redundant. Now, if one of us could *fly*, that would be something we could have used.

"Would it be easier to carry him if he wasn't on the stretcher?" Petra said, with a nod towards Tilly.

"I don't know," Maratse said. "I'm not sure we should risk it."

He sat on his heels for a moment as the three of us looked at Tilly, each lost in our thoughts, variations, no doubt, along the lines of how much easier it would be if Tilly was conscious.

"We don't even know if his neck or spine is injured," I said.

"We can't risk it." Maratse turned up the volume on his radio and keyed the button to transmit. "This is Maratse, ETA on helicopter?" He let go of the radio and stared at his feet as we waited for the response to crackle through the speaker.

"The weather is clearing. Maybe twenty or thirty minutes."

"Make it twenty," Maratse said, "and we'll be on the port side of the ship."

"Affirmative."

Maratse scrambled to the edge of the stairwell. He looked up at the cupboard with the firefighting equipment, and then down at the restaurant below. I shuffled to a position behind him as Petra peered over the edge. We each saw the crests of the waves splashing at the restaurant's panoramic windows. Twenty minutes sounded like an awfully long time, all of a sudden.

"Did you see the fire hose?" Maratse asked, pointing at the cupboard above us. "Is it the thick kind, or flat?"

"Flat," Petra said. "I think. But it's not a rope, David."

"It might have to be." He pointed along the corridor, towards the door leading onto the deck. "We have two choices," he said. "Either we try to climb up to that door…"

"I don't think I can climb with one hand," I said.

Maratse nodded. "Or we use the hose to help us back down to the restaurant."

"Go back down?" Petra shook her head. "Closer to the water. We need to get up, and away…"

"Piitalaat."

"We can't go *down*, we'll drown. We need to go up." Petra scratched her neck, digging her nails into her skin, tracing red welts from beneath her chin to the top of her jacket.

"Piitalaat," Maratse said, as he reached out to take her hand. "It's okay."

"No, it's not. We can't go down."

"Going down is easier," he said, with a nod to Tilly on the stretcher.

"If we go down, we die," she said. "We'll drown…"

"But if we go up and fall, we might break our legs, or our necks."

Petra jerked her hand, trying to tug it out of Maratse's grip, but he held it firmly to her side.

"Piitalaat?"

"What?"

"Listen," he said. "If we go down, we can walk through the restaurant to the deck." He paused at a long groan from the *Gjøa*, as she tilted another metre towards the surface of the sea. "Then we use the railings like a ladder to climb onto the side of the ship." He nodded at the corridor. "This is flat. It would be like climbing the face of a glacier. Nothing to hold onto. The railings will be our ladder." Maratse looked at me, and I nodded.

"Yes," I said. "I'm ready."

Petra closed her eyes for a moment as she wrangled her lungs into producing regular breaths, rather than the shallow rapid ones that began when Maratse first suggested climbing down towards the sea.

"Okay," she said. "I'm okay. But it has to be now. I don't want to wait any longer."

"Good," Maratse said. "But you have to get the hose."

"What?"

Maratse pressed his back against the first two steps of the stairs, linked his fingers, and made a step with his hands. "One foot here, the next on my shoulder..."

"I can't do that."

"*Iiji*," he said. "You can."

"I'll fall."

"I'll catch you."

"Then we'll both fall."

Maratse dipped his head briefly before a broad smile spread across his lips. The green glare of the emergency lighting marking the way to the upper deck, danced in Maratse's eyes.

"That's the alternative," he said. "The fastest way to the restaurant."

"You're crazy," Petra said.

"*Iiji*."

Petra took a moment. She held her breath for a

second, pressing her palm against the bulkhead as she looked down at the restaurant and then up at the cupboard. I guessed it was a metre above Maratse's head, and then a bit more to the cupboard handle – the hinges faced downwards, towards us. Petra would have to stand on Maratse's shoulders, leaning outside of the stairwell.

"Okay," she said, as she exhaled.

I expected another short discussion, or at the very least, a last exchange to confirm the plan. But Petra just bit her bottom lip, gripped Maratse's jacket sleeves, and stuffed her right foot into his hands. Maratse gave Petra the boost she needed to place her left foot on his shoulder. She leaned out of the stairwell, slapping her palm against the bulkhead as she reached for the cupboard. Maratse grunted as Petra knocked her right knee into his nose.

"Quickly," he said, nodding at me.

I reached up and pressed my right hand against Petra's buttock, pushing her closer to the wall of the stairwell as Maratse gripped her ankles.

"Both hands," he said.

"My wrist…"

"I don't care."

I bit back a stab of pain and pressed my splinted palm next to my other hand, pushing against Petra's body as she cursed and fumbled with the cupboard above us.

"I need to get out there," she said.

"I can't hold you out there," Maratse said.

"Lift my right foot."

"Piitalaat."

"Just do it. I'm nearly there."

Maratse slid his fingers beneath the sole of Petra's right foot, pushing upwards, as I changed my grip to the backs of her thighs, and then her calves as she climbed up and out of the stairwell.

"Almost," she said. "I've got my fingers on the door. I just need another ten centimetres…"

The click of the cupboard door opening was almost lost beneath Petra's scream as she tumbled out of the stairwell, her fingers clawing at the end of the hose as she tried to grip it.

"Piitalaat," Maratse shouted.

He reached for her, leaning out of the stairwell – too far out. I grabbed the back of his belt, and held on as he stumbled, slipping to one knee as Petra dropped down the corridor towards the restaurant. The hose wheel swung out of the cupboard like a rescue winch on a helicopter, trembling as the hose rattled through the wheel.

Petra's scream stopped as she expelled all the air in her lungs, just as the hose caught at the end of the wheel. I looked over the edge of the stairwell to see Petra swing at the end of the hose, penduluming into the corridor running parallel to the restaurant. She disappeared. We heard a thump and the crash of something that sounded like glass splintering, and then the bright red plastic nozzle swung back into view. I yanked at Maratse's belt as he lunged forwards.

"No," I said.

"Piitalaat…"

"I know, but wait…"

It felt like the longest time I had ever waited for anything, but in reality, it was perhaps only a few seconds, maybe fifteen, before Petra called out that she was okay. Ten seconds after that, and she crawled into view, picked herself up, and squirmed the soles of her boots onto the back of the leather bench bolted to the deck beside the restaurant door.

"I'm okay," she said.

Petra ducked her head as the nozzle arced above her. She caught it, jerking her arm as she slowed its momentum, until the fire hose hung in a straight line from the cupboard to the restaurant. The nozzle was less than a metre above the thick glass window separating the restaurant from the corridor.

"Are you hurt?" Maratse asked.

"Bruised," Petra said. "I'm shaking, but I'm down." She gave a weak *thumbs up*, brushed her hair out of her face and smiled. "Your turn."

"Stretcher first," Maratse said, as he pulled the hose out of Petra's grasp.

The nozzle bumped against the sides of the corridor as Maratse pulled it up and over the lip of the stairwell. He took a bight of hose, looped it around the bottom of the stretcher, and then again in the handhold above Tilly's head.

"It's going to be heavy," he said.

"I know."

Maratse lifted the stretcher and slid Tilly's feet over the edge of the stairwell, while I hooked my arm around the banister and gripped Maratse's belt with my good hand. The stretcher scraped against the side of the corridor until Maratse took a tiny step forward. With the tips of his boots over the lip of the bulkhead, Maratse lowered Tilly down the corridor, pausing every once in a while, at Petra's direction. Maratse's arms trembled until Petra shouted that she had her fingers on the bottom of the stretcher, and again, calling out the remaining distances in centimetres until Tilly was safely positioned on the back of the sofa outside the restaurant. I let go of

Maratse as Petra untied the knots holding the stretcher.

"You're next," he said, as he pulled the hose back up the corridor.

"You're sure you can hold me?"

"Do you see anyone else?"

It could have been humour, but one could never tell with Maratse, at least not with any degree of certainty.

"I'm joking," he said, as he fashioned a sling from the hose, looping it around my legs and shoulder before tying it at my waist. "Try to keep your feet on the wall or the floor on the way down, but don't bounce."

"Okay."

Maratse gripped the hose. "Ready?"

"Yes," I said.

Maratse walked back to the banister, braced himself against it and took up the slack. I nodded that I was okay, and he told me to start when I was ready.

"But soon," he said, as the *Gjøa* exhaled another metallic groan.

The first few steps were the hardest, as I slipped, scuffing my knees and my palm as I pushed away from the sides of the corridor.

Petra called out the distance from below. Shouting so that Maratse, hidden inside the stairwell, could gauge how far I had to go, and for how much longer he had to hold me.

"Almost there," Petra shouted, and then, quieter, "You're doing fine."

"Maratse's doing all the work."

"Good," she said, smiling as she reached up to grab my foot and steady my descent. "He's being punished, remember?"

I laughed the last metre or so, and it felt good. I just

hoped that, in Maratse's case, the punishment didn't fit the crime.

I looked up and shouted that I was down, as Petra worked on the knot at my chest.

"It's tight," she said, struggling to get her fingers between the folds of the hose.

"Probably my weight."

"I'll have to cut it." Petra shouted for Maratse, waving at him as he leaned out over the lip of the stairwell. "I can't undo it."

"Cut it," he said.

"Then it'll be too short," she said.

Petra stumbled as the *Gjøa* fell another metre onto her starboard side.

"No time," Maratse said. "Cut it."

Part 6

I was left with almost two metres of fire hose in my hands once Petra cut me free of the makeshift sling Maratse had tied around my body. Maratse would have to drop the last few metres once he was finished with his descent. It didn't sound like a lot and it didn't stop him climbing down, but I worried that he might twist his ankle or worse as he fell. After all, I had managed to break my wrist just coming down the stairs. But as Maratse kept reminding us, there was no time.

The last four metres were not the problem, I realised as the wheel holding the fire hose buckled and ripped free of the bulkhead. It slammed into the opposite side of the corridor as Maratse fell half the distance between the stairwell and the restaurant. Petra held her breath and I watched, unable to move or speak as he hurtled towards us, gripping the hose above his head, flailing with his feet until the spokes of the wheel caught on a door handle. The hose jerked tight, stretching Maratse's arms above his head as he held on, slamming his body into the side of the corridor. He rebounded into the space between the walls again, until he swung just ten metres above us.

"Climb down, David," Petra shouted. "Now, before it breaks."

Maratse grunted something in reply, then twisted his leg around the hose, wrapping it around his ankle, as he climbed down, jerking his hands down the hose until he was close enough for us to reach him.

"It goes all the way down now," Petra said, as Maratse's arms began to tremble. "Just keep going."

Petra guided Maratse onto the narrow strip of the bulkhead beneath the restaurant windows. She held him tight as he caught his breath – deep breaths to try and counter the adrenaline that coursed through his body. Maratse pressed his forehead against Petra's.

"*Qujanaq*," he whispered.

"You're welcome."

I turned away for a second as Petra pressed her hand to Maratse's cheek.

"Exciting, huh?" she said.

"*Iiji*."

"You're pleased you came?"

"You didn't give me a choice, Piitalaat," Maratse said. "I was being punished."

"Well," she said, with a light slap of his cheek. "Consider yourself on probation now, for good behaviour."

Maratse's shoulders shook and I wondered if his muscles were still reacting to the effort of lowering us down the corridor, followed by the adrenaline kick associated with falling. When I saw his face, I realised he was laughing, but not for long. We were running out of time.

"Okay," Petra said, as she grabbed the end of the stretcher, curling her fingers around the aluminium tubing to one side of Tilly's feet. "Let's get outside."

I took the other side of the stretcher, ignoring the pain in my broken wrist, letting it dangle by my side as Maratse lifted the top of the stretcher and we entered the restaurant. We took it slowly, stepping on the edges of tables, coordinating each step, pausing at every creak of metal as the table legs shifted a millimetre or so under our weight and Tilly's. Maratse led us from one row of tables down to the next, as we inched towards the rear of the restaurant and the deck, the starboard side of which was now just five metres above the water.

Maratse paused at the door onto the outside deck of the balcony, pointing at the railings.

"Like a ladder," he said. "We climb up and around the inside. Use the joins in the bulkhead like steps when the railings stop."

"We'll have to climb out at some point," Petra said, looking up.

I followed her gaze, focusing on the climb, and not the sea below us.

"*Iiji*," Maratse said. He unbuckled his lifejacket, pulling the straps off his shoulders.

"What are you doing?" Petra asked, as Maratse strapped his lifejacket around Tilly's body, passing the straps through the aluminium tubes and buckling it at the back of the stretcher. "Now you don't have a lifejacket," she said.

"Neither do you." Maratse pointed at the tattered lifejacket hanging from Petra's shoulders. She unbuckled the straps and shrugged it off. "Use the straps as a loop," Maratse said, taking the useless lifejacket from Petra's hand and cutting the straps into two lengths with the knife on his belt. He put his knife away and attached one long loop to each end of the stretcher. "If you lose your grip, grab the straps."

A sudden rush of wind behind us turned our heads, just as the swing doors to the kitchen burst open. Flames licked at the edge of the door and the crackling of the fire, competing with the wind gusting just outside the glass door leading to the restaurant balcony.

"Let's go," Maratse said. He gripped the stretcher, sliding it across the table closest to the door, and letting it pivot for a moment as he reached for the door handle. The door jerked in his grasp and he let go of the handle, letting the wind slam the door flat against the outer bulkhead. The handle cracked against the side as Maratse straddled the door and reached back for the stretcher, pulling Tilly towards him as the wind tugged at his jacket and hair, and the flames licked at the restaurant tables behind us.

"Wait," Petra said. "Let me get below it."

She waited for a nod from Maratse, and then let go, climbing down to stand on the edge of the next table beneath the stretcher, then guiding the stretcher to Maratse, as I shoved the other end. Tilly stirred as the wind tugged at his hair, but his eyes stayed closed. His skin paled in the fresh gusts from the sea, but the colour in his cheeks returned as soon as Maratse dropped down below him, tipping the stretcher to pull Tilly out of the door and onto the exposed deck.

"Give me your hand," Petra said, reaching out for me, as I held onto the loop at the end of the stretcher. "It's okay. Maratse's got the weight. Let go, and we'll get you outside."

I took Petra's hand, squeezing it perhaps more than necessary, as I clambered over the tables and took the last leap to the door. The metal was cold and slippery. I let go of Petra and lowered myself onto a step of sorts, where two sheets of steel had been riveted together. Petra crouched in the door frame above me, nodded that she was ready, and then lowered the end of the stretcher, bending down and holding it at the very end of the loop, until Maratse told her to let go. Tilly's feet jerked under the straps as the end of the stretcher hit the solid section of steel before the railings curved up and away from the sea.

Maratse waited for us to climb down to him, oblivious to the crackle of the flames in the restaurant and the shrieking of the wind as it stirred the sea into evil white horses – steeds of the devil.

"This is going to be tough, wet, and cold," he said.

Maratse went first, climbing and pulling the stretcher as we pushed from below. The *Gjøa* creaked and shuddered with each new wave, and the wind pushed her closer and closer to shore. We stopped for short breaks of a few seconds, followed by a longer one when Maratse's radio crackled with an update.

"We have a boat in the water. The helicopter will be in the air in five minutes."

Maratse clicked the radio twice to respond, and then waved at the crew of the black RHIB from the *Knud Rasmussen*. I thought I recognised the driver, and almost cringed at the thought of being rescued for a second time by *Marineoverkonstabel* Ea Albæk.

"Ready?" Maratse said, raising his voice above the wind.

We climbed along the railings, and when we ran out of railings, we slid our boots onto the steps formed by sheet metal joins, bolted in place. The surface paint was slick, but I found if I twisted my foot until my ankle protested, I had a better purchase, enough to lean into the side of the ship and lift as much as I could with my free hand.

"You've done well," Petra shouted, reaching up to tap my foot. "But you can't do anymore. Can you hold on here?"

"For how long?" I asked, cursing myself for not just saying *yes*.

"Just until we get the stretcher over the side. Maybe five minutes."

"I can wait five minutes."

"We'll come back for you."

I nodded as I slipped my hand through a smooth rectangular hole in the bulkhead. I pinched the metal in the crook of my elbow, ignoring the cold as I pressed my palm against the outer side and my body against the other. The metal was cool on my forehead as I rested it against the side, listening to Petra and Maratse curse the stretcher over the side of the ship, fighting against the wind and the freezing spray of the sea, until the wind whipped their voices away from me and I was alone.

I ignored the crash of the sea below me, shrinking into a bubble that neither the wind nor the waves, and not even the flames could penetrate. It could have been hypothermia, but the effect was euphoric. I felt warmer than I had been since we left the restaurant. I shuffled my free hand up my body to try and open the zip of my jacket, just to let a little air in, just to cool down. It was so hot, all of a sudden. Maybe the flames had reached me, close enough to warm my body? It wasn't so bad. It was almost a comfort. Everything was better now, although the loose strap of my lifejacket was a bother, slapping me across the face.

"Wake up."

Another slap. I lifted my hand, ignoring the pain in my wrist to wave the strap away, maybe even grab it. The slaps were getting harder.

"Open your eyes. Wake up. You're not going to die here."

Was I dead? I felt the opposite of dead. Death was the cold that prickled the hair on my arms. Death was the roar of the wind that tugged at my jacket sleeves, whipping and snapping at my trouser legs and cuffs. Death was that final hard slap that made me open my eyes.

"You have to move," Petra shouted, pressing her face into mine. "Move."

She grabbed a fistful of my jacket and tugged me forwards.

"Climb," she shouted, dragging me behind her as we climbed out and over the side of the ship. The wind twisted the long tail and loose strands of her hair, whipping them about her face as Petra used the rungs of the ship's ladder welded into the side, pressing her body close to the rungs as she gripped each one, pulling me up the ladder behind her.

I finally opened my eyes, wide enough to see where we were, to fix our position on the side of the ship, about fifteen metres above the water, working our way towards Maratse. There was something in the air, thudding and thwacking above us, but I couldn't see it. But below, close to the side of the ship, but holding a discreet distance, was the black rigid hulled boat from the *Knud Rasmussen*. The driver shone brightly in her red survival suit, as did the two crewmen, one in the bow, and the other on the starboard side, pointing and shouting directions and distances, or so I imagined; the wind stole their voices.

"Nearly there," Petra said.

I looked up as she reached for the strap flapping in the wind above her. Maratse held the other end. He must have taken it from the bottom of the stretcher, using the other end to tie Tilly to the last rung of the ladder above him. Petra waited for the wind to blow the loop towards her, grabbing it as it brushed her fingers.

I looked up as she tugged at my hand. I lifted my foot, felt it slip on the cold wet rung of the ladder. I reached out with my other hand, grabbing at the rail, only to slide and bang my wrist. I retched, caught the bile in my throat, and lost my footing on the ladder, slipping onto the smooth side of the ship, and pulling Petra with me.

"Piitalaat," Maratse shouted.

I could hear the strain in his voice as Petra and I swung beneath him. I felt Petra tighten her grip on my hand, digging her nails into my skin as she held on, kicking at the side of the ship, the rubber soles of her shoes squeaking as she sought purchase – a rivet, the lip of a window, anything.

I looked down at the sea below, the grey waves, less than fifteen metres away. I had been on longer water slides at theme parks. If I let go, I would slide into the water. I might even be lucky, keeping my head above the surface long enough for Ea Albæk – yes, it was her – to click the RHIB into gear and come pick me up.

It was the only option.

I lifted my head to look up at Petra, saw the fear in her eyes as she stared through the tangle of her hair spinning and twisting in front of her face.

"I'm not letting go," she said.

"It's the only way."

"No," she said. "I won't let go."

She didn't have to.
Maratse did.

Part 7

The cold clutched at my chest as I slid into the water, pressing like a vice around my ribs. I forgot all about the pain in my wrist, focusing instead on breathing, or at least trying to breathe as the lifejacket auto-inflated on impact, and Petra crashed into the sea beside me. I felt her grab my shoulders and we both ducked under the surface, choking on the water rushing into our mouths. Then a rumble of something broke through the crash and gurgle of water and the whipping of the wind. I saw a black shape pressing through the waves towards me, felt rough hands pinch my skin as they grabbed at my collar and the straps of my lifejacket, yanking me out of the water, exposing me in a broadside to the wind as they heaved me once, halfway up the side of the boat, and then again, onto the deck and just below the grasp and clutch of the wind.

I heard excited chattering, voices cut and pasted on the wind, as the driver clicked the gears back and forth, twisting the boat as the crewman left me to lean over the side, kicking me with their heels as they lunged for Petra as she broke the surface. They dragged her over the side, flopping her onto the deck and pumping the sea out of her lungs until she rolled onto her side and vomited. The crewmen dressed us both in heavy blankets, tugging woollen hats onto our heads, stabbing and cutting the lifejacket away from my body to close the gap between the wind and my wet clothes.

Petra called out for the driver to stop the boat, as we pulled away from the *Gjøa*.

"Maratse," she said.

"We can see him," Ea said.

"We can't leave him."

"We won't. Look."

Ea pointed up at the grey, flurry-filled sky above the cruise ship. The Danish Navy's Lynx helicopter hovered above Maratse, turning almost gracefully in the wind, as if the roar of the thunder of the rotor blades was enough to challenge the wind gusting across the Greenland Sea, pushing the *Gjøa* closer and closer to the coast.

A crewman swung out of the helicopter's cabin, dangling at the end of the winch as he was lowered to the side of the ship. It all seemed so familiar, and I wasn't surprised when Maratse helped the crewman secure Tilly to the winch. Maratse waited on the side of the ship as the crewman returned to the helicopter, spinning outside the cabin until the winchman helped him slide Tilly inside the cabin.

Petra ignored the helicopter, staring directly at Maratse, alone on the side of a sinking ship, leaning into the wind, sidestepping when a gust caught him off guard.

I saw what Petra didn't, tapping her arm and pointing at the Danish *Knud Rasmussen* as it towed the Icelandic Coast Guard cutter into deeper water, away from the stricken *Gjøa*, the pride of the *Arctic Horizon* fleet, now reduced to little more than a challenging and expensive salvage mission.

Petra glanced in the direction I pointed, then turned back to watch Maratse, as the helicopter adjusted position, and the crewman was lowered for a second time to collect him. She waited until he was onboard, and the winchman closed the cabin door, before nodding to Ea that she was ready. Ea turned the bow of the RHIB into the oncoming waves, quartering them at half speed as she picked a gentle but insistent course back to the *Knud Rasmussen*.

The Lynx flew above us and we watched it land on the aft deck of the Danish patrol ship, compensating for the rolling deck until it slammed down onto the landing pad, long enough for the crew to secure the helicopter and for the pilot to cut the power and apply the rotor brakes.

Maratse was waiting on deck when we pulled alongside. He nodded at me, before tugging Petra out of the crewman's arms, holding her close, brushing wet strands of hair from her forehead as she shivered in his arms.

"You let go," she said.

"I had to."

"You heard the helicopter?"

"*Eeqqi*," Maratse said, shaking his head. "But I saw the boat."

Petra's lips stretched into a weak smile as she pressed her forehead against Maratse's chest. He curled his arm around her shoulders and walked her towards the door, guiding her stubborn and cold feet over the lip of the door and inside the ship.

"You have to go inside now," the crewman said. "You're going hypothermic."

"I know," I said. "I just want a last look."

The crewman stood beside me as I gripped the railing and stared at the cruise ship lying on its side just off the coast of North East Greenland. We had been lucky. The ship had been practically empty, but for a skeleton crew and a gaggle of journalists.

"Very lucky," the crewman said, and I realised I must have spoken my thoughts aloud. "But next time it might be for real, if you know what I mean?"

"For real?"

"A cruise ship full of passengers, with our assets – ships and helicopters – spread all around the coast of Greenland. It could take hours to for help to arrive. Maybe a helicopter could get to the ship within an hour – minimum, depending on where it is and how much fuel it can carry, but even then…"

"One helicopter," I said.

"You really are on your own out here," he said. "I think it's hard for people to appreciate that."

"Yes," I said, although I felt I had a much better appreciation now than just a few hours earlier.

The crewman took my arm. "You need to get inside," he said. "Hypothermia is no joke. And we need to take a look at your wrist."

I nodded and let him guide me inside the ship, felt his hands lift my stubborn legs over the lip of the door, just as Maratse had done for Petra. I had been in the water for less than a minute, I couldn't imagine what I would be like if I had been immersed just one minute longer.

What was it Tilly had said? Something about the only real use of a lifejacket was to help rescuers locate the bodies.

"*Souls*," I said. "Not *bodies*."

Epilogue

The smell of fish drying on oil-smeared wooden racks is one of the most authentic smells of Greenland. Add the buzzing of flies around the thicker chunks of meat – halibut, or Arctic cod, maybe even the black Greenland shark – and you've got the beginnings of an Arctic symphony of the senses. There's the deep blue sea, the bright pink sky, the white icebergs, and the browns and greens of the land, late summer, that is, not winter. Then more sounds, such as the cawing and croak of the ravens, the whine of the sledge dog, and the immature growls of the puppies rolling at one's feet. Don't forget the children, scuffing their shoes in the grit as they chase each other around the drying racks. The keen wind carries all of these things – the sharp and salty fish odours, the raven cries and the giggles of children, together with the bite of the wind as it brushes against your skin, drying the moisture in your nose, as you zip up your jacket in anticipation of winter.

That's my Greenland, very far and very removed from ships colliding in the sea. Like I said at the beginning of this story, I write *people* stories, not *Titanic* stories, which is just as well, as the Danish Navy turned down my editor's request to have me participate in

SAREX. I never got further than Tasiilaq, the largest town on Greenland's east coast, and the starting point of many of my adventures with Constable David Maratse.

It should come as no surprise then, that he found me sitting on a bench nestled between heaps of bright green and orange fishing nets, buoys and markers, punctured fibreglass hulls and a cheerful gang of eleven children playing tag between the fishing racks.

"I saw your name on the list," he said, as he sat down on the bench beside me.

"The list of journalists for SAREX, you mean?"

"*Iiji*," Maratse said, as he lit a cigarette. "Your name had a big black line through it."

"Probably because of what happened in Tunnulik," I said.

"Probably."

Maratse waved at a little girl as she giggled her way past us, dragging a length of fishing line caught in her shoe. She said something in east Greenlandic, pointing at her shoe and pouting, until Maratse rolled his cigarette into the gap between his teeth and got off the bench to help her. She twirled around him until they were both tied up in the net. Maratse placed his hand on the girl's head, holding her like one holds a spinning top, while cutting them both free of the net with his knife. The girl shrieked and ran away, holding her arms wide as the wind ruffled her imaginary feathers. Maratse slipped his knife into the sheath on his belt and returned to the bench.

"So," he said, nodding at the pages of notes in my lap. "What are you working on?"

"It was supposed to be an article about SAREX. But, as you know, I couldn't go." I paused for a second to wave at the girl as she flew another low-level sortie past our bench. "My editor doesn't know yet. But I decided to try a story instead."

"Fiction?"

"I suppose so," I said. "It's about two ships colliding during the SAREX exercise. You're in it," I said. "And Petra."

Maratse grunted, then finished his cigarette. He took the papers from my lap, rearranging them according to the numbers I had pencilled at the top of each page.

"I'll get some coffee," I said, leaving him to it.

It took longer than expected to find take-away coffee. I was about to give up when, walking back towards the bench, a young mother thrust two porcelain mugs of thick black coffee into my hand and nodded towards Maratse.

"Thank you," I said, as I took the mugs.

The woman smiled, curling her hands through the long black hair of the low-flying girl pressed against her leg. The girl wrinkled her nose when I spoke to her in Danish, and then twisted as her friends called to her. I carried the coffee to the bench, slopping it over my fingers as I stumbled around a stray clump of fishing net.

"What do you think?" I asked, as I put the mugs down on the bench between us. "It's all made up, of course."

"I was being *punished*," Maratse said.

"Yes," I said. "Because, well, I don't know *why* you were being punished exactly, but that would be how she would do it."

"Petra?"

"Yes." I paused, looking for the right word. "Because you don't *need* anything, Maratse." He frowned and I continued. "I mean, look at this," I said, with a wave of my arm that took in the fish racks, the bloody and oily hulls of the hunter's boats, a patch of blood on a rock, and two seagulls fighting over a string of seal entrails floating in the water close to the shore. "That's *you*, not some plush cruise ship. That's why it would be a punishment, for you," I said.

"Hmm."

Maratse shuffled the papers into a pile and handed them to me.

"*Hmm*," I said. "That's all?"

"*Iiji.*"

"Then you don't think it could happen? It's just fiction?"

Maratse turned the coffee mug on the bench, and then picked it up. He said nothing for a few minutes, content to just stare out to sea and drink his coffee.

"It's not fiction," he said, as he rested the mug on his thigh. "That's the problem. It could happen. Maybe like you said, maybe worse. Maybe not tomorrow, but soon. It will happen soon."

"You're sure about that?"

I almost added: *can I quote you on that?*

"Pretty sure," he said.

Maratse finished his coffee. He stood up, tugged a packet of cigarettes from his pocket and tapped one into his hand.

"Publish it," he said.

"You think so?"

"*Iiji.* Maybe it will make someone think."

"What about the parts with you?" I said. "And Petra?"

"Publish them too," Maratse said, grinning as he stuffed the cigarette between his lips.

"Will she read it?"

Maratse nodded. "I'll make her," he said. "It'll be her punishment."

THE END

CHRISTOFFER PETERSEN

Author's Note
_____

I have three notes I'd like to share about *Asiaq*. I'll start
with the factual one.

I like to explore Greenlandic issues, both cultural and
contemporary, in each of Maratse's novellas. *Asiaq* is no
different. I can't remember just how many times I have
heard a Danish Naval Commander comment on a
potential disaster of *Titanic* proportions just waiting to
happen in Greenland. As the Greenland tourist trade
grows, so does the potential for a disaster at sea. While
tourism is an essential part of Greenland's economy, the
resources and assets needed to respond to such a disaster
are limited, not least by the geography and the scale of
Greenland, the world's largest island.

Many cruise ships sail responsibly. But, as the sea ice
retreats due to global warming, more and more cruise
ships will likely consider Greenland to be an attractive
means of expanding their cruise ship packages, in an area
normally restricted to vessels with strengthened hulls
designed to cope with ice. This will place further
demands on Greenland's resources, both on land and at
sea. When cruise ships visited the areas I lived and
worked in, in the north of Greenland, the passengers and
crew on just one ship easily outnumbered the residents on

the land. Even Nuuk, with a population of app. 15,000 people, can experience an extra two or three thousand people on certain days each summer.

It will only take one cruise ship disaster to bring the current situation into sharp focus, and more than one journalist will likely use the word *Titanic* as they report on the incident.

My second note is more personal, in that I have deliberately added an epilogue that could be compared to a dream sequence, i.e. did the story told in *Asiaq* actually happen? If we ignore for a moment, the fact that I am writing fiction (albeit based on a lot of facts), I would say that for the sake of continuity, the events in *Asiaq* did not take place, apart from Maratse and the journalist meeting in Tasiilaq. Clearly, it would be difficult for Maratse and Petra not to at least mention this event in future books, such as *Seven Graves, One Winter*. They haven't as yet, and they are unlikely to.

Which brings me to the third and final note.

I write Maratse's novellas because I want to explore many of the different aspects of Greenland, its people, their culture and traditions. There's far too much to stuff into one novel, or a series of novels, without it reading like a guide book. So, I hope you will forgive me this indulgence. More so, when writing the novellas – limited as I am by a chosen length – I find that some of the stories could easily be fleshed-out into full novels. I like the idea of expanding on some of these stories, *Asiaq* being one of them.

I hope you enjoyed *Asiaq*, and once again, I hope you'll forgive my indulgence.

Chris
August 2019
Denmark

P.S.

The cadets I taught at the Greenland Police Academy participated in SAREX during my year in Nuuk, just like the cadets in the years above and below them. The stories and photos they shared on their return from the exercise were just amazing. And, yes, Canadian Para Rescue Jumpers did parachute into the Greenland Sea to stabilise the "victims".

Camp Century

~ A short story of secrets and scandal in the Arctic ~

Part 1

It's hard to imagine a typical journalistic assignment in Greenland, and, as experience has shown, there is often a crime associated with each of them. Why then should a geological field trip to Camp Century prove any different? Of course, I knew it wasn't a run-of-the-mill geology expedition, there were far too many colourful characters in the mix, including the technical advisor, Arika Jones, chosen for her knowledge of glaciers and ice, but none the less interesting for her Australian Aboriginal background. I could write a whole article just about her. But my editor wanted more than a personal profile piece. He said there was something strange about the expedition, that when he saw the list of expedition members, he just knew something was going on. I had to admit, the American historian in his fifties, together with his Greenlandic companion, piqued my interest. The fact that they went missing on the third day after their arrival at camp just added to the intrigue. That was when Arika took over.

"It's likely," she said, "that they have fallen down a crevasse. Lærke has organised the teams for the search."

I shuffled my feet in the snow as Lærke Toft Hansen, the Danish leader of the geology expedition, took a step forward. She ran a gloved finger down a list of names tacked to an old-fashioned clipboard, calling out the leaders before assigning two more people to each team.

"I realise we're still getting to know each other," she said, brushing her grey fringe to one side. "So, it makes sense just to remind you who we're looking for." She hugged the clipboard to her chest, pressing the air out of her thick winter jacket, and said, "Most of you know Josh Shellenberger." She paused at a quick wave of smiles that spread between the expedition members – twelve in all, including me, but minus Josh and his companion. "Josh is our resident historian, and I know he has entertained many of you with his Camp Century stories on the flight up here. But you might not have met his companion, Serminnguaq Satorana. She joined us at Thule Air Base. Both of them are in their fifties. And now, obviously," she said, with a nod to the group assembled in front of her, "they are missing. It might be they just went for a walk…"

"And broke the first rule of camp," Arika said. "No-one leaves camp without permission and they can only get that by signing out with either Lærke or me in the main tent."

It struck me that Arika was perfect for the job of safety advisor, but I did wonder if she was capable of relaxing, and how she would react when the expedition members actually started to venture beyond the camp perimeter.

"Yes," Lærke said. "But if they have just gone for a walk, then I'm hoping they haven't gone far."

"They don't need to go far to get into trouble," Arika said. "This area is riddled with crevasses, and God knows what else," she said, fiddling with the film badge dosimeter hanging from a lanyard around her neck.

I checked my own badge and wondered just how

much radiation was too much and how I would even know? I had missed Josh Shellenberger's impromptu talk about radioactive waste from Camp Century. One of the younger members of the expedition had put him on the spot. But I remembered Arika's comments about shifting ice, and how the waste had been spread over a massive area since the reactor was removed in 1967. I looked at my feet. I could be standing on top of radioactive waste without even knowing it. Arika's voice dragged me back to the job at hand as she checked everyone's climbing harness, the ropes connecting each team, and the ice axes we carried.

"You're a journalist?" she said, as she tugged at the loop at the front of my harness.

"Yes."

"Danish?"

"Yes."

"Your government has been awfully quiet about this, hasn't it?"

"You mean the radiation?"

"I mean the camp, the radiation, the lack of clean-up, the deniability – yes," she said. "I mean all of those things."

"Well," I said, wondering where to start.

"Are you going to write about it?"

"I'm going to write about something. That *is* why I'm here."

Arika stopped fussing for a second and stared into my eyes. I had never met an Australian Aboriginal before, but despite being wrapped up in high-tech climbing equipment, including a shapely short-waisted winter jacket with a high collar, Arika seemed to radiate something of the desert, together with a passion for the land. The thick black curls of her hair escaping from the fleece hat sitting snug on her head, bobbed as she sniffed in the cold, before tapping me on the shoulder so that she could check the back of my harness.

"I don't like having civilians on an expedition," she said. Her fingers dug into the back of my thighs as she untwisted one of the leg loops.

"You're a civilian."

"I meant *non-climbers*."

She tapped me again and I turned around. I waited for her to say something more, but she just shook her head.

"Will I do?"

"You'll do," she said. "Just stay with your group."

I watched Arika walk away, crunching the surface layer of snow beneath her winter climbing boots. She was shorter than me, but she walked tall. That was the impression I got. It was the impression she left on everyone, according to the chatter in the camp at night. I shrugged and found my team, letting the leader clip me into the rope that would keep us all secured and stop the *civilians* from wandering off. His face was hidden behind polarised goggles, the kind that reflect a petrol rainbow of colour, but he smiled, and I felt instantly more welcome, despite my lack of climbing experience. I was just about to ask his name, to check if I had remembered correctly. He could have been Brian or Roger. But when someone shouted that they had found Josh, it didn't seem to matter anymore.

The four teams trudged across the ice to a dip just beyond the camp perimeter. The ice flowed in a classic tongue shape down towards the west, its tip curling sharply to the north, revealing a hollow beneath the curl.

Lærke called out for everyone to wait, which we didn't, and to be careful, which we weren't. Only Arika's sharp tongue stopped anyone from walking too closely to the body sprawled in the snow ahead of us.

Arika unclipped her safety line and approached the body, one hand on her ice axe, digging it into the surface of the ice with each step. She stuffed the axe into the ice to one side of the body, before she knelt beside it to turn it over.

Even at the distance Arika had us wait I recognised Josh Shellenberger's face, although his cheeks were more flushed than I remembered, as if he had struggled for air during his last moments.

"He's dead," Arika said. She turned to look over her shoulder at Lærke. "You're going to have to call someone."

Lærke nodded. She tugged at the chest pocket of her jacket, her fingers fumbling with the flap and the zip, before she pulled out a satellite phone. "Yes," she said. "Yes, I'll call."

We all watched as she tried to remove her gloves and hold the satellite phone, but even though it was cold, it seemed to me that her fingers were shaking far more than the temperature warranted.

"Let me help you," I said, taking a step forward.

"Wait."

I felt a tug at my waist as Brian – I think that was his name – unclipped my safety line. I nodded my thanks and then strode the last few metres to Lærke.

"I'm sorry," she said. "My fingers..."

"It's all right." I turned the phone in my hand and unlocked the keypad.

"Do you really think he's dead?"

"He looks it," I said. I pulled up the pre-set list of contacts and found the number for the emergency services. "I guess we need the police? If he's dead…"

"He's definitely dead," Arika said. She nodded at the phone in my hand. "You may as well talk to them. You're Danish."

"They speak English," I said, but she had already moved away, drawing Lærke with her. Arika spoke in hushed tones, but I heard words to the effect of *be strong* and *leadership*, and then I decided to make the call.

Once I had explained the situation to the control centre, and they had ascertained that no-one was in danger, and that the victim was indeed dead – Arika confirmed with a sharp nod of her head when I repeated the question in English – they said they would send a local police officer, and that we shouldn't touch the body before they arrived. I confirmed that we would wait in camp, but it never occurred to me that we were still missing one person. The shock of discovering a dead member of the expedition stunned everybody with the same numbing paralysis.

Arika left two people with a radio by Shellenberger's body and herded the rest of us back to camp. It was only when we heard the approach of a helicopter two hours later, that someone remembered that the Greenlandic woman was still missing.

"Oh my God," Lærke said. "What if she's dead, too? I can't cope with that."

The helicopter – an American air force Huey – flared above the area designated as the camp landing pad, marked with oil drums and flags that flapped in the downdraught from the Huey's rotors. Arika raised her hand to protect her face from the swirl of ice that blistered through the air, but I caught a glimpse of the determined set of her jaw. Even in the face of forgetting the missing Greenlander, she still captured the image of the strong leader, quite the opposite from the unassuming face of the police officer who climbed out of the helicopter. He tucked his hands into his jacket pockets as soon as he was clear of the helicopter skids, walking with the quiet confidence that I remembered and looked forward to each time I met Constable David Maratse. He nodded once at me before turning to look at Arika.

"Someone has died?" he said, in his scratchy English.

"Josh Shellenberger," Arika said. "He's fifty-three. American. He's the expedition historian…"

Maratse nodded towards the camp. "Where?"

"Right," she said, and I hid my smile as I realised it was the very first time she had seemed flustered. She recovered in less than a second, set her jaw to maximum, and pointed to the far side of the camp. "I'll take you there."

I tagged along behind them, wondering when or if Arika would call Maratse a *civilian*, or if locals were exempt? The pilots and crew stayed with their helicopter as we walked through the camp and then up and over the rise that hid Shellenberger's body. Arika led the way, waving the two young geologists away from the body as we approached. She stopped a few metres away, waiting for Maratse to examine Shellenberger.

"They could have sent a more talkative cop," she whispered, as I joined her. "This one's a moody bugger."

I stifled a laugh, and said, "You have no idea."

Maratse crouched by Shellenberger's body, looked to both sides and then rolled it over.

"Aren't you going to photograph the scene?" Arika

asked as Maratse went through Shellenberger's pockets.

"Are these your footprints?" he said, pointing at the snow.

"Yes."

"And those?" Maratse pointed behind him.

"Yeah, they're mine."

"Did you kill him?"

"No." Arika started to say more but stopped when Maratse shrugged.

"You can move the body," he said. Maratse picked up Shellenberger's wallet and a small leather notebook that he had pulled out of the cargo pocket in the dead man's jacket. It looked like a diary. It looked old. Maratse walked back up the slope and handed it to me. "Your English is better than mine," he said.

"Is that it?" Arika said. "What about cause of death?"

Maratse shrugged. "The doctor will need to determine that."

"But what happens now? Do we just carry him onto the chopper and…" Arika reached out to tug at Maratse's jacket as he turned away. "Hey. Where are you going?"

Maratse waited for the two geologists to lift Shellenberger's body, and then crouched once again in the snow. He dipped his head, staring at the hollow beneath the curl of smooth glacier ice that turned north. He dropped to his knees, and then scraped at the snow with his hands.

"What have you found?" Arika said, as she jogged down to where Maratse lay flat in the ice.

"A tunnel," he said, as he wormed his way inside.

Part 2

Maratse crawled deeper into the snow tunnel until the only thing I could see of him was his boots. He would have gone further and beneath the tongue of ice if Arika hadn't grabbed his ankles and pulled, until he squirmed out of the hole to glare at her.

"There's someone inside," he said, brushing the snow from the front of his jacket. "Who else is missing?"

"A Greenlandic woman," Arika said. "I don't remember her name." She grabbed Maratse's sleeve as he ducked towards the tunnel entrance. "But I can't let you crawl in there. It's not safe." Arika pulled at Maratse's arm until he brushed her away. "You have no idea if the floor is ten metres or ten millimetres thick. You could be crawling into a crevasse. Let my team dig into the tunnel. We'll make sure it's safe. Then you can explore, if you really think someone is inside."

"*Iiji*," Maratse said. "Someone *is* inside."

I believed him. I had seen that look far too often to doubt him. But a crease of impatience played across Maratse's face as Arika explained her position on the team, and her responsibilities. It had nothing to do with her being a woman in charge. Maratse just didn't like waiting. But I wasn't sure that Arika understood that.

"You're questioning my authority?" she said, at

another crease across Maratse's brow. "If you are, then I suggest you go back to the camp, talk with Lærke – the expedition leader. She can show you the papers. If that doesn't satisfy you, you can call the government of Greenland, or the Danes, whoever you want. I don't care." Arika jabbed a finger at the entrance to the tunnel. "But no-one goes inside that tunnel until I've made it safe. Is that understood?"

Arika's face bloomed with a deep heat – I could feel the energy charging out of her body. But she didn't waver from her position. I wondered at her jurisdiction, and the point at which Maratse's jurisdiction would trump Arika's, but the thought was brushed aside as Arika called the camp on her radio and set her team in motion. Everyone else was to be confined inside the camp perimeter, until she said otherwise.

"Including you, Constable," she said, as she lowered her radio.

Maratse took one last look at the tunnel entrance, and then started walking back to the camp. "Hurry," he said, as he passed Arika.

I walked beside Maratse all the way. He said nothing more, but twice he paused to look back at the tunnel, and a third time when Arika's team rushed past. The shovels they carried reflected the spring sunlight and the ropes they wore slung over one shoulder bounced at their hips. Maratse watched them for a few seconds more, and then continued into camp.

One of the pilots from the helicopter waved to Maratse as we walked inside the camp perimeter. He tapped his watch and said something about *flying hours*, before promising to return should Maratse need the helicopter.

"We'll take the body to the morgue at Thule Air Base. The doctor can look at him, but we'll keep him on ice until you get back. I guess he'll have to be repatriated as soon as the investigation is over."

"There's another person missing," Maratse said, tapping a cigarette out of the packet and into his hand. "We might need to coordinate a search."

"It looks like you've got plenty of people here already," the pilot said. "But keep us posted."

Maratse nodded, lit his cigarette and rolled it into the gap between his teeth. He stuffed his hands into his pockets as the pilot walked away. I followed him to the main tent, drawn by the chatter of the diesel generator, briefly masked by the helicopter's departure. I stood quietly and froze slowly, as Maratse finished his cigarette, breathing a silent sigh of relief when he opened the canvas fly of the tent and nodded for me to go inside. Maratse followed a second later.

The inside of the communal tent was arranged with four long tables with low benches on either side. I sat at the table closest to the gas heater, like the ones I had seen in the outdoor seating areas of Copenhagen cafés in autumn and early spring. Maratse spoke with Lærke, drawing her away from the computer to give her an update on the situation, and to glean more information from her about Josh Shellenberger and the missing Greenlander. I listened with half an ear and then remembered the diary Maratse had given me. I peeled off my gloves and tugged the diary out of my jacket pocket, removed the thick rubber bands that kept it closed, and then put it on the table.

The cover of the diary opened flat, as if it had been read many times. The pages were lined with a faint blue ink that stretched across each of the creamy yellow sheets of paper. The pages were yellow at the edges. Several of them had greasy stains that showed the writing from the other side. I closed the diary, ran my fingers over the thick cover, then opened it to the first page, searching for a name. I smiled when I saw it, and again when I found the date of the first entry. I looked up as Maratse's shadow fell on the table. He sat down and nodded at the diary.

"Is it Shellenberger's?"

"Yes," I said, "but I don't think it was Josh Shellenberger's diary. It might have been his father's. Look at this name." I pressed my finger to a name printed in tight capitals in the middle of the first page. "Frank Shellenberger," I said. "And the first entry is from May 2nd, 1960."

"Hmm." Maratse frowned as I turned the diary for him to see. "1960?"

"From what Josh told us the other night, the American Engineers – from the army – finished building Camp Century in 1960." I pulled the diary back across the table and flicked through the first few pages. "Josh said that army servicemen rotated back to America after 180 days. If Frank was here in 1960, it could be that he was one of the first men to actually serve inside the finished base."

"In 1960?"

"Yes," I said.

I opened the diary to the first page and started to read. Maratse stopped me. He pointed at the coffee urn on one of the far tables.

"I get the coffee, you read," he said. "Aloud."

"You want me to translate?"

"*Eeqqi*," he said, as he walked to the coffee urn. "Just read slowly."

I ran my fingers along the first few lines of Frank's diary, getting a feel for his handwriting. When Maratse returned with the coffee I was ready.

"I'll just start then," I said.

Maratse nodded.

"Okay then." I plunged into the first entry, catching up just as Frank did, after what he described as a hectic start *with a heck of a rush.*

May 2nd 1960
I'm still gettin' used to the light – all the time. So bright. But there's no time to get used to anythin'. Yesterday, and the day before that, was all about gettin' the "heavy swing" ready. The swing is a tractor train that leaves Tuto (Thule Take-off) headin' for Camp Century – the city beneath the ice. A heavy swing has the most tractors – they look like an amphibious tank on caterpillar tracks – and each tractor pulls a trailer carryin' a wannigan. The wannigans are wooden boxes – some of them have bunks, others are offices, then there's the science laboratories – those guys have got a few bunks stuffed inside of them, too. But Captain Walker told me two days ago – or was it three? It's so hard to keep track, what with there bein' no night 'n' all, but, anyways, Captain Walker said I was drivin' one of the tractors. I was going to be a "cat skinner". I figured I would be, but he's given me the last in the swing – says I have to be on my guard. What he actually said, word for word, was: "It's a big responsibility, Frank. I think you can get the job done. What about you? Do you think you can do it, Frank?" Naturally, I told him "Yes, sir!" and he shook my hand

and told me to carry on. Everyone round here likes the Captain, they even call him Eugene when they're off duty, and sometimes he hears them, and he acts like it's alright, "but not too often, boys". That's what he says. "Not too often."

"He sounds young," Maratse said, as I paused for a sip of coffee.

"I think he is. Straight out of training, and then sent to Greenland – off on an adventure." The writing was infectious, and I grinned at the thought of a young man arriving at what must have been strangest place he had ever seen. Maratse tapped the diary, and I continued, skipping a few pages of details about camp life until Frank's handwriting changed, as if he was writing in a hurry, or with great excitement. As I started to read, I realised it was the latter.

I was just gettin' settled in the seat of my cab when I saw her again. The Eskimo girl. The boys say she's from the camp down by the harbour, that she's lived here all her life. They say she's about seventeen, and gosh, she sure is pretty. It's the eyes – dark brown, but alive, like traffic lights – no, that's not right, but I don't know what to call them, or how to call them. Just that they're bright, flashin', and if she catches you – with those eyes, well, it's like lightnin'. I've been struck a few times already, includin' that first day I got off the ship. She was waitin' on the dock, gettin' in the way, but no-one told her to move. She just sat on one of those huge wooden crates of equipment, kickin' her heels against the side, wearin' those sealskin boots over a pair of cotton pants. She had a t-shirt on – nothin' more than that, and there was ice on the water, snow on the ground, and she's just sittin' there, as if it was the height of summer, if you please. Well, I noticed her – all the boys noticed her, what with all that black hair curlin' in the wind, and her smile. Then she comes by, wanderin' past the swing, and I'm in my tractor and she waves – at me. Not the others. (Well, she might have waved at them, but I don't care – she looked in my cab and waved at me!) Eugene – Captain Walker – he said we was to treat her nice, but to ignore her. "Don't encourage her," he said. But all I did was wave, and then watch her, from the cab. I heard one of the old timers say she wasn't wearin' a bra, that they probably didn't have bras in the Eskimo village. Well, I looked, and he was right.

"I think Frank is falling in love," I said.

"*Iiji.*" Maratse looked at his watch and then stood up. "I want to see how far they've got."

"Okay," I said. I started to close the book but stopped when I saw the next few lines. I lifted my hand, gesturing for Maratse to wait. "Just a little more," I said.

Once we got the heavy swing into motion, I forgot all about the girl. I had to concentrate all of a sudden. Drivin' those big cats on the ice, keepin' a good distance from the next tractor – not too far, not too close – it tuckers you out, I'll say. Then when we called it quits for the night, after just five miles, I was the first inside the wannigan. I found my bunk and I was just pullin' off my woollens, about ready to strip down, and then I heard it – I heard a giggle. That girl took a whole year off my life when she slid out from under the bunk. Then she hit me with that smile, and those eyes. Well, I forgot all about what Eugene said. I couldn't ignore her. She was right there. So, I put my hand on my chest and I said, "I'm Frank." I pointed at her and asked her what her name was. She looked on me like no girl has ever looked on me before, and she said, "Nialiánnguak." It took some time for me to say it, then longer to spell it. But that's who she is, and now I have to figure out how to tell the Captain. He's not going to be best pleased, but I don't think he'll turn us around. And that's alright by me.

Part 3

"Before you go," Lærke said, as Maratse walked towards the door. "I've got the information you wanted." Lærke waved Maratse over to her desk, and then stood up so that he could take her seat at the computer. "That's his application," she said, reaching around Maratse to open Josh Shellenberger's details on the screen. "I couldn't find much about the woman, other than her name." Lærke tapped the screen in the section reserved for *comments*. "I think you'll be able to say her name better than I can, Constable."

"Serminnguaq Satorana," he said. "She's from Qaanaaq, or maybe Savissivik."

"You know her?"

"I know her surname."

"There's not much more about her," Lærke said. "But as she required no transportation, and would meet us here, I didn't think much more about it. We've all been busy," she said. "It took some time to get the expedition approved. The government – all of them – seems to get concerned whenever an independent expedition wants to visit this area." She tapped the radiation badge on her jacket. "This probably has something to do with it."

"Hmm," Maratse said. He scrolled to the top of Shellenberger's application and pressed his nose close to the screen to read the text. He nodded and leaned back when Lærke suggested he enlarge the document. "*Qujanaq*," he said, settling back in the chair.

I leaned over Maratse's shoulder, quietly translating words when he pointed at them. According to his resume, Shellenberger was an accomplished historian with several publications to his credit, a host of articles in leading historical journals. He had one particular area of interest that formed the basis of his application to join the expedition, and that was the building and operation of Camp Century. A personal note confirmed what we had already gleaned from the diary, that Shellenberger's father had been stationed at Camp Century in the early years of its operation, before it was decommissioned.

"We're mostly concerned with ice," Lærke said, when Maratse nodded that he was finished. "It's unusual for a geology expedition to have any members other than scientists, students, and climbers. You've met Arika Jones," she said, with a quick glance at Maratse.

"*Iiji.*"

"She was against adding Shellenberger to the team, but I convinced her that his name would give us access to additional funds."

"And did it?" I asked.

"Oh yes," she said, gesturing at the inside of the tent and the gas heater. "We're not used to such luxury."

I was tempted to ask if Arika had approved my place on the team, but Maratse brought the conversation back to Shellenberger and his companion.

"What about Serminnguaq?"

"I remember meeting her, but she hardly said more than a few words. I'm not sure anyone spoke to her, actually."

"Where did she sleep?"

"She shared a tent with Josh."

"What was their relationship?"

"I couldn't say." Lærke looked away, as if she was remembering something. "They didn't seem close, but there was definitely something going on. The few times I saw them together, it always looked like they had just had an argument. But they held hands, more often than not."

"Shellenberger was fifty-three," Maratse said. "What about Serminnguaq?"

"I don't know," Lærke said. She lowered her eyes, and then said, "I'm sorry, I'm not good at guessing the age of Greenlanders'."

Maratse shrugged. "Neither am I." He pointed at the computer, and said, "Can you send me a copy of this?"

"Yes, of course."

Maratse tugged a grubby business card from his wallet and handed it to Lærke. "The email is on the back."

"And what are you going to do now?"

"Find Serminnguaq," Maratse said, as he stood up.

I stuffed the diary into my jacket pocket, pulled my gloves on and followed Maratse out of the tent. He smoked as we walked back to the tunnel, stopping on a rise just beyond the camp perimeter to look down at Arika and her team digging below. They had been busy since we left them, slotting aluminium slats into the grooves of metal posts screwed into the ice, shoring up the sides of the tunnel as they dug deeper under the ice.

"If anyone was in there," I said. "They would have found them by now. Don't you think?"

Maratse said nothing until he had finished his cigarette. He nodded at Arika's team, and said, "She won't come out until they are gone."

"You mean Serminnguaq?"

"*Iiji*." Maratse stuck his hands in his pockets. "We should wait. Tell me about Frank."

"You mean read some more of his diary?"

Maratse nodded, and I tugged the diary out of my pocket. The rubber bands were tricky to remove with gloves; Maratse did it for me. He held the diary for a moment, turning it in his hands, before handing it to me to read. I started with the entry for the following day.

May 3rd 1960

Captain Walker was mad alright, and the drivers, too. He made us all sleep in the one wannigan. It was warm but cramped like a doghouse. It smelled like one too. Nialiánnguak was supposed to sleep in the crew's wannigan all by herself, but she snuck into ours late in the night. If anyone heard her, they didn't say a word. I just kept real quiet, but I didn't sleep a wink, I could feel her body pressing against my toes. I couldn't say if it was her back or her belly, and I don't rightly know if I should even guess, but I knew she was there the whole night, right up until the first driver woke, and she snuck out, hightailin' it back to her wannigan before anyone saw her. Captain Walker called a meeting over breakfast. He said we'd come too far to turn around, what with the weather 'n' all. And, he said, it wasn't safe to send one tractor back to base, even if he wanted to. He said he would call a helicopter to come and pick her up. But then one of the old timers said that wouldn't work, because they were strugglin' to adapt them to the cold. The new helicopters – the H34s – needed to be polar-oiled, and they hadn't done that since unloadin' them from the ships. It would be one, maybe two days before they were flyin' – weather dependin'. Two days! Weather dependin'. I hoped the Captain couldn't read minds, because I was giddy over the thought of that little Eskimo girl warmin' my feet for one or maybe two nights. I had no other intentions – cross my heart and tell my mother – but she was about the prettiest girl I ever seen, and I didn't mind that she stowed away on the heavy swing. I didn't put her there, I didn't ask her, but I didn't want to send her away either. Of course, the Captain can't read minds, but he can read faces. He said "Shellenberger," not Frank, so I knew I was in trouble. He said, "She's your responsibility. She rides in your cab. You keep her safe. And no screwing around." The men laughed at that, and I don't know whose face was redder – mine or the Captain's. He didn't mean anythin' by it, but the men laughed all the same. Some of them even complained that it wasn't fair, or that it wasn't smart to put her in my charge, but I was determined to do my best, and I told them so. One man laughed so hard at that, I stuck my face in his and, I declare, I would have hit him so, if the Captain hadn't intervened. He sent us back to our tractors, and he sent Nialiánnguak back to mine. I was still fumin' over that lard ass with the smart comment, but I wouldn't show it. I opened the door for Nialiánnguak, and I found her a big jacket. She disappeared right inside it, and I laughed. She laughed too – the sweetest sound I ever heard. Then I started the tractor – all the tractors started – and the heavy swing swung into motion. She chatted the whole time, and I didn't understand a word. But my jaw ached from smilin', all the way until the next stop, and then some.

I closed the diary, snapped the rubber bands around it, and tucked it away. I had a good idea where the story was headed, and I questioned Captain Walker's reasoning behind putting young Frank Shellenberger in charge of Nialiánnguak. But maybe he didn't have a better alternative? I couldn't find a reference to Frank's age, but I guessed he was in his early twenties. Stuck in a tractor cabin with a pretty *Eskimo girl*. Frank's diary had all the ingredients for a romantic novel, but the next instalment would have to wait, as Maratse walked down towards the tunnel.

Arika met us at the entrance. Her jacket hung from a ski pole, and heat steamed from her body. She shook her head and pressed her palm into Maratse's chest as he tried to walk around her.

"We've only just begun."

"You've dug the entrance," Maratse said.

"We've widened it and made it safe."

"And you've found the way in?"

"Sure, but you have to understand, if this is part of one of Camp Century's tunnels, it's been twisted and deformed for fifty years, moving down the ice cap towards the sea. It's just pure luck that there's a hole in there at all. My guess is, from what we've seen, it must have been one of the larger halls that's been compressed into something like a tunnel. We found splinters and the odd plank of wood, probably from a building they left inside. But it's not a tunnel, not like you think it is, anyway."

"But there is a space inside," Maratse said. It wasn't a question.

"Yes," Arika said. "But no-one's going in there, until it's safe." The snow crunched beneath Arika's boots as she shuffled back a step. "Look," she said, with a softer inflection in her voice. "If anyone's hiding inside there, they're too scared to come out right now, what with us working right outside. There's a gap, so there's air." She paused to look up at the sky. "I don't like the looks of those clouds, but we'll keep going until we have to stop. I can send someone for you as soon as we're done. How about you wait back at camp?" She looked at Maratse and then turned to me. "I could use a weather report, and a fresh battery for the radio."

"I can get it," I said, pleased to have an excuse to go back to the tent. I had been cold in Greenland before, colder than this, but standing around on the ice chilled my bones. Maratse, as usual, seemed wholly unaffected.

"Do you have an extra shovel?" he asked.

"Yes," Arika said.

"Then I'd like to dig."

Maratse walked down to the tunnel entrance as Arika gave me her radio. She explained where the spare batteries were and said that Lærke would be able to provide the weather report.

"One more thing," she said, touching my arm as I turned to leave.

"Yes?"

"Do you know him? The Constable?"

"Yes," I said. "We've met several times."

"Is he always like this?"

I had an idea what she meant, but a simple *yes* or *no* never seemed adequate when describing Maratse. I could try and explain his passion for the land, and how that was only ever exceeded by his love for his people, but it was never something that he expressed, certainly not though emotions. Maratse showed his feelings through his actions. He struggled with waiting when waiting seemed counterproductive, and yet he never hurried, especially when the weather, the land, or the sea – more often than not, the ice – determined otherwise. But when people were in danger, Maratse's patience had a limit; it was just difficult to know when he had reached it. I settled for the easy answer.

"Yes," I said. "He's always like this."

Part 4

It took less than ten minutes to grab a new battery for Arika's radio. Lærke promised to give Arika a weather report as soon I took the radio back to her. I lingered for a second as Arika took the radio. Maratse's jacket hung on a ski pole next to hers and he dug alongside the young members of Arika's safety crew, swapping the occasional grunt, as was his way. I could have helped, and I'm ashamed to say I didn't, but I felt my time could be better spent finding out what happened to Frank and Nialiánnguak. I told Arika I would be in the main tent if she or Maratse needed me. I think she heard what I said, but it was lost in the storm warning filtering through the radio, intensified by the urgency in Lærke's voice. I shuffled across the ice, stepped into the camp perimeter, and then hurried to the main tent. I told myself that I was doing my bit to help find out what had happened to Josh Shellenberger, and guiltily helped myself to another mug of coffee. The tent was warmer than when I fetched the battery – more people. I found a spot on a bench furthest from the heater and started to read.

May 3rd 1960
The visibility got real bad after lunch. Captain Walker had warned us about a storm, and once the snow started

we slowed to a crawl. Normally, a heavy swing could get from Tuto to Camp Century in about 3-5 days, but a storm would mean double that, at least. We crawled to a stop, but Captain Walker told us to stay in our cabs, just in case it cleared. We kept the engines runnin' for heat. Then his voice crackled over the radio orderin' us to stay in our cabs, because he didn't want to lose anyone in the storm. I couldn't even see the hood of my own tractor, let alone the next tractor in the train. I was goin' nowhere. Now, Nialiánnguak started chatting, and I chatted right back. I think we both told different stories, with a pause to let the other nod or say somethin' as if we understood what the story was about. For my part, I tried to explain why they called the drivers "cat skinners", but they don't have cats in Greenland – leastways I had never seen one – and they don't have caterpillars neither. So when I mimed that I was skinnin' a cat, or bunched my finger like a hungry caterpillar, she just laughed, and darn near melted my heart. Of course, it got strange then. Not strange, but hot. I almost turned down the heat. Then she shrugged off that jacket, and then she pulled off her t-shirt, and the old timers were right – they don't have bras in Greenland. I couldn't take my eyes off of her. Even the thought of Captain Walker bangin' on the side of my tractor, or hollerin' for me to get out and roll in the snow to cool down... I had those thoughts, but they didn't last. Because then all I could think of was that pretty little Eskimo girl, how Captain Walker had ordered me to look after her, then ordered us to stay in our cabs, and then, well he didn't order anythin' else, but what else could I do? I don't mind sayin' that I was not experienced in these kinds of things, and I don't mind admittin' that I was right afeared in the start, wonderin' if I would do things right, if I could do what she wanted. But Nialiánnguak knew what to do. She knew plenty. She helped me through the whole thing – helped me out of my clothes until we were both buck-naked, then helped me some more. I don't remember ever feelin' that way before, but of course, my heart – I remember it beatin' so loud, so fast, I remember strugglin' for breath. I must have been red-faced, so bad she slowed down. I remember rollin' down the window, just needin' some air. That felt better, and then we... well we did it then. I don't know as to what I can say. No more than that. It was better than I had heard – better even than I had dreamed. What with the storm n' all, it was probably better than anythin' I would ever do or feel again. I held her through that storm. I held her right close. Then, when we started to cool, well, I just tugged that old jacket on top of us, and we stayed there through the night until mornin'. The wind didn't let up. We stayed there the whole next day too. Plenty of food in a tractor – and plenty to do, now that the Captain ordered us to stay there.

I closed the diary, sipped my coffee, and then took a moment to look around the tent. The sides of the tent snapped, sometimes billowing when a big fist of wind punched against them. I hadn't noticed, and thought nothing more of it, until one of the geologists said something about me being an *old timer*, and I laughed at that.

"No," I said. "Just got stuck in my book."

"What book is that?"

I didn't have an answer for that. It seemed inappropriate to tell the other members of the expedition that I was reading the diary Maratse had found on the body of Josh Shellenberger. They mentioned him in between gusts, and I suddenly felt awkward.

It was Maratse who saved me, together with Arika and her safety crew as they blustered into the tent, snow swirling from their bodies in the wind, until the last member of the team stepped inside and secured the flap of the tent. Maratse grunted something about coffee and stalked towards the urn as soon as Arika unclipped him from the safety line she had attached to his utility belt.

"I told him we would start again, as soon as the wind dropped," Arika said, as she sat down at my table. "But he's convinced she's inside the tunnel, and that we're wasting time."

"We are," Maratse said, as he sat down next to her. He pushed a mug of coffee into her hands, and then sipped at his own.

"This wind," Arika said, "is coming right off the top of the ice cap. There's no way we can dig in this." She sighed as she warmed her hands around the mug. "The snow will blow into the tunnel. If this lasts for too long, we'll have to dig it all over again. You're sure she's inside?"

"*Iiji*," Maratse said, with a nod of his head.

"But how can you know that? For certain."

"I don't," he said. "But where else can she go?"

I waited for Arika to respond, and then, when she didn't, I turned the diary towards Maratse and ran my finger along the last line on the page.

"Frank slept with Nialiánnguak," I said.

"Slept with?"

"Had *sex* with," I said. "They were stuck inside the cab of his tractor, in a storm. The whole night. So far, anyway."

"Who's Frank?" Arika asked.

"We think it's Shellenberger's father."

"That's the diary you found in Josh's pocket?"

"Yes. Maratse gave it to me to read."

"My English is a little rusty," Maratse said. "He helps."

Arika turned her head slightly, just enough to add a little more weight to the look she gave me. "It's weird," she said. "I'm getting this strange vibe that the two of you are like Holmes and Watson, or something, only not so smart." Arika laughed. "Sorry. You know what I mean."

I did, and I could see the similarity. But while Maratse was too quiet and too reserved to ever reveal just how smart he actually was, it was the setting that ruined any further similarities. The wind thumping against the sides of the tent. The twenty-four-hour sunlight tempered and filtered by the snow clouds, and the temperature, plummeting as the wind leached it out of our bodies, forcing Lærke and one of the expedition members to change the cylinder for the gas heater before the wind showed any signs of abating.

"What happened next?" Maratse asked, with a nod at the diary.

I turned the next page, pausing as the geologists from the surrounding tables and the diggers from Arika's team crowded onto our benches, with more rearranging the tables behind us so that they could sit close, leaning in against the wind.

"This is Josh's father's diary. Frank Shellenberger – Josh's dad – has just spent the night in the cab of his tractor," I said, bringing them all up to speed. "He was on his way to Camp Century. He's a young man, and there's a young Greenlandic woman with him." One of the geologists made a gentle *ooh* sound, and we all paused, wondering if it was appropriate until Lærke cleared her throat and announced we were out of gas.

"So, huddle up," she said, with a nod to me. "If you're ready?"

I pressed my finger to the page, pitching my voice a little higher as I started to read.

May 4th 1960

It was foggy the next mornin' – a real pea souper. I had a fright when Captain Walker banged on the side of the tractor. Nialiánnguak was sleeping in my arms. I gave her a quick shove and sat bolt upright in my seat, just as the Captain climbed up onto the runnin' boards and opened the cab door. He sniffed at the air as he climbed in and I wondered if he guessed somethin'. I had thought about what I might say if he asked. In fact, I had thought about it all night. Nialiánnguak had snored – she even snored pretty – and I hadn't slept one bit. I thought about my heart too, and if I was to get that excited every time I was with a woman, then I might want to see a doctor about it, although just what I would say to him, I don't know. Anyway, Captain Walker said somethin' about the fog, but that we would keep driving. I said I didn't know as to how we would do that, and he just smiled and pointed at the roof. "I'm sending someone to your cab," he said. "This fog is a ground fog, just a few metres high. If you stand on the roof you can see the top of the wannigan in front of you. You'll drive and Smith will give you directions." He told me to repeat the instructions back to him, and then he got ready to leave. But before he went, he cast a quick look at Nialiánnguak. Her jacket was open, and the Captain and me could see the creamy brown skin of her belly, and a bit more besides. She didn't seem to care. She just smiled. Then I saw how her hair was wild and tangled, and I felt that grip on my heart again, and I got all red-faced. In fact, Captain Walker was so concerned he forgot all about Nialiánnguak. Or, at least I thought he did. On his way out of the cab, he picked up her t-shirt and tossed it into her lap. He muttered somethin' before he slipped out of the cab and dropped down to the ice. He left the door open, and I wonder if he did it on purpose, because when I leaned out to grab the handle and close it, he was right there by the door, lookin' up at me. I'll never forget what he said, and I'm not sure he meant to say it, but it made me laugh anyways. Captain Walker looked up at me, and he said, "Carry on, soldier."

"I get it now," said the young geologist who had asked me what I was reading. "It's better than the books I've got in my tent."

"It's real, too," said another geologist. She thumped the arm of the woman next to her. "Imagine being stuck inside a cab on the ice cap, with a bloke. Nothing to do. There's a storm blowing…"

They carried on, embellishing the story as they sat out the storm, emptying the coffee urn, making a new batch, sharing similar stories, then agreeing that nothing came close, until someone prompted Arika to tell the one about the dentist in the cable car.

I closed the diary and made myself comfortable, as Arika worked her face through a series of protestations, saying that she wasn't going to tell that story, and then, a second later, that she would, as soon as there was more coffee. Someone reached over the huddle of geologists and thrust a fresh mug into her hand. Arika cleared her throat, but I didn't hear a word of what she said, I was too busy watching Maratse as he quietly wormed his way through the expedition crowd and slipped out of the tent.

"Serminnguaq Satorana," he said, as I ducked under the tent flap and joined him outside. The wind whipped at the collar of my jacket and I cupped my hands over my ears, leaning close to Maratse as he continued. "The woman in the tunnel."

"Yes?"

"She's Frank Shellenberger's daughter."

Part 5

The wind cut through the folds of my jacket, penetrating the zip, stuffing cold air into the pockets of space under my arms, around my ribs, anywhere it pleased. Even Maratse dipped his bare head into the wind, and I followed him, one hand tucked into the back of his utility belt, as he led the way back to the tunnel. The wind had dumped fresh snow inside the trench dug by Arika and her team. We waded through it. The going was slightly easier, on account of the trench wall providing some, if not a lot, of protection from the wind. Two shovels marked the entrance to the tunnel. Maratse tugged one out of the snow and pressed it into my chest. He picked up the other one, pointed to his right, then dug to his left. I joined him, digging and scraping the snow clear of the entrance, cursing the wind as it swirled spindrifts of snow down my neck, or lifted the skirt of my jacket to stuff more snow up my back. I remember the first trickle of sweat being a welcome relief, a kind of rebellion against the cold wind. But Maratse warned me not to get too hot, placing his hand on my arm, and pulling me onto my knees, out of the wind.

"We can get inside now," he said, scraping snow to form a lip around the entrance. He slid the shovel inside the tunnel, and ducked, ready to follow it.

"You don't think we should wait?"

"Serminnguaq has waited long enough."

Maratse squirmed over the lip of snow and through the entrance. I watched his boots disappear, then followed him, only to return for the snow shovel the second Maratse noticed I had left it outside. When I returned, I was surprised to see that the sunlight filtered through to a certain depth in the ice, providing more light than I had expected. It was enough to see several metres further into the tunnel, to a point where it twisted sharply to the right. Maratse crawled on ahead of me and I followed.

It grew darker at the turn, but mercifully warmer, and quieter. The wind rasped and raged at the surface, but for all we could hear or feel of it, it might has well have been but a breeze, sinking to our knees as the air cooled inside the Greenland ice cap. I remembered something about climbers digging snow holes and pressing ski poles through the roofs, waggling them every now and again to keep a tube of air flowing into the snow hole. Even if we had ski poles, the ice was too thick, too deep and too strong to chip a breathing hole through it. I just hoped Serminnguaq had not gone too far. It crossed my mind that it would be hard work to drag a body through the tunnel. Perhaps that was what urged Maratse on. He crawled faster, until the ice floor curved away beneath us, opening like a huge tongue sticking out of a cheeky child's mouth. I bumped into Maratse, blinked in the gloom, and then gasped at the sight of wood timbers, some of them warped, others splintered, but arranged in a wall that might have been the side of a building erected inside the original Camp Century. It didn't seem likely, but there was no other explanation. I closed my fingers around the radiation badge fixed to my chest pocket and wondered if we were exposed to radioactive waste, and what that would mean, how it would affect us. Perhaps that was the story my editor wanted me to write? I think he suspected the climbers on the expedition to be secret activists, and Arika fit the profile perfectly – displaying a fierce dedication to her trade, and a deep respect for nature. But whatever the official or unofficial reason for the expedition, it was the human aspect that had brought Maratse to the ice cap, and *that* was the story I would write – to hell with my editor.

"There," Maratse said, pointing into the darkness.

I followed the direction of his finger, and then saw a dark shape curled on the ice. The ceiling was higher than in the first part of the tunnel, and I could sit with my chin on my chest. I did so as Maratse crawled towards the shape that I guessed was Serminnguaq. She had found a good hiding place, although I wondered how long she could stay down here without freezing or suffocating. I thought about hypothermia, struggling to remember if it was slurred speech, or shivering that came first. But there was nothing wrong with Serminnguaq's speech when Maratse reached her.

The hollow beneath the ice cap echoed with a sudden roar of hoarse Greenlandic; she flung a torrent of consonants and so very few vowels at the walls. I could hear the grief wrapped around each word even though I couldn't understand the words themselves. Maratse's voice was soft by comparison. I heard him repeat the same word again and again, variations of pitch, but always soft, until Serminnguaq's shouts became sobs, and each heave of her chest rocked her body closer to Maratse, until he had her in his arms, and he held her so tight, too tight to shout.

Even then, with my chin buried against my chest, and the cold seeping through the seat of my trousers, chilling my spine, I couldn't help but wonder at the change that came over Maratse each time he came in contact with his people. Old or young, it didn't matter. Maratse, the taciturn constable, wore his badge on his jacket but his heart on his sleeve. I tilted my head to watch as he held Serminnguaq, rocking with her as she sobbed, until her tears glistened, cooling in tiny streams on his jacket. Maratse beckoned for me to come closer as Serminnguaq started to talk.

Her first words were a confession of murder – at least, that's what Maratse told me, as he translated her Greenlandic into Danish.

"Make a note," he whispered, and I patted my pockets for a pencil, having already learned that pens were susceptible to the cold. But I had no notebook, and I said as much. "The diary," Maratse said.

"Of course," I said, nodding as I tugged it out of my pocket. It seemed fitting to record Serminnguaq's story in Frank Shellenberger's diary, especially if she was his daughter. I turned to the blank pages at the back, and made a note of the date, in the same style as Frank started each of his entries, and then I started writing, as Maratse translated.

I was born in January, in a hunter's cabin somewhere on the coast between Thule Air Base and Qaanaaq. My mother, Nialiánnguak, had been sick, but she had been travelling with her father – my ata – by sledge. No-one knew she was pregnant – she was slim, with a tiny belly, and the winter furs hid the rest. But when she started to complain of cramps, ata got scared.

They were coming home, but he stopped at the cabin. Her waters broke on the snow. Ata carried her into the cabin. He lit a fire in the stove, then helped her out of her furs. I was born within an hour of them arriving at the sledge. The first light I saw was flame light, and the only warmth was my mother's skin, but that soon cooled as she died shortly after giving birth.

I was grateful when Maratse paused. The image of a lonely cabin beneath the black sky of winter, flame light licking at the wax paper windows, was strong, all the more so for hearing about it inside a tunnel wormed into the ice cap. I thought of Serminnguaq's first hours, and the grief her grandfather must have felt at losing his daughter. I imagined him carrying Nialiánnguak's body to the sledge, securing her to the wooden thwarts with cords of sealskin. How would he carry the baby? How would her keep her warm? Maratse explained as Serminnguaq continued.

Ata carried me inside his furs, pressed against his bare chest. He told me this every January of my childhood, how he tied a length of cord around his waist, pinching the sealskin smock to his body. He said he had to breathe through his mouth, exhaling to one side, for fear of his breath freezing on my face. He sledged back to Qaanaaq – it was closer – and he found a cousin to look after me, while he searched for a place to bury my mother. The ground was too hard to dig – frozen. They made a coffin, and my mother lay in it through the winter, on top of a low roof, until they buried her in mid-July. I stayed in Qaanaaq, growing up alongside my second cousins, greeting my ata every spring when he travelled across the ice from Thule. When I was six years old, I went with him, back to Thule. He took me up to the Americans. He told them that one of their soldiers was my father. They turned him away, said he had no proof. But he pointed at my fair skin and told them to find a Greenlander with white skin like his granddaughter's. When they ignored him, he got angry, and they escorted him back to the village looking out on to what they called North Star Bay, in the shadow of Mount Dundas. And that was where I lived then, because ata got sick, and he died late that same summer. I was six years old. I never knew my grandmother, but a friend of hers took me in, and I lived with them until they sent me to school in Upernavik. I didn't go back to Thule for many years. But when I did go back – I was twenty years old – the woman who had cared for me said a man had come looking for me, that he had left something for me.

Maratse stopped translating as Serminnguaq pushed at his arms and pointed at the diary in my hands. She switched to Danish, and said, "The man left me a letter, but I couldn't read it."

"Was that man Josh Shellenberger?" I asked.

"*Aap,*" she said. "He came all the way from America to find me. He carried that diary with him."

"Did you read it?"

"I can't read it. I can't read English. But it doesn't matter anymore. He is dead. I killed him."

I wasn't ready for the shriek that followed as Serminnguaq's character altered as if she had flipped a switch. She railed against Maratse's chest with her fists, forcing him backwards, before she turned on her knees, revealing a small, dark hole in the ice behind her. She slid inside it, kicking at Maratse's hands as he clutched her ankles. She kicked free and slid out of sight. Maratse lurched after her, and he would have followed if I hadn't grabbed him by the shoulder, dropping the diary onto the ice beside me, as I pulled him away from the hole.

"You don't know where it goes," I said. "You don't know if you will be able to get out."

"That doesn't matter," he said.

"Yes," I said. "Yes, it does. It matters, Constable, because you don't have to die to save her. That's not how this works."

"You don't know how this *works*," he said.

"No, but Arika, back at the camp – she knows *ice*. You know *people*. If you work together, you can still save her, without getting trapped beneath the ice."

For a moment I thought he was going to shrug free of my hand and plunge into the darkness after Serminnguaq, but he settled, relaxing his shoulders as he leaned his back against the tunnel's icy wall.

"She is ashamed," he said. "She feels guilty. She thinks she killed Shellenberger."

"But you don't think so?"

"*Eeqqi*," Maratse said, with a shake of his head. He looked at the diary, pointing as I picked it up. "The answer's in there. I will go for help. You keep reading."

Part 6

May 4th 1960

Smith crawled onto the roof just as Captain Walker said he would, and he steered us in the tracks of the tractor in front of us. We kept goin' for eight hours, stoppin' twice to refuel, before Captain Walker called it a night. All the men bunked down in the wannigan to give Nialiánnguak some privacy. She didn't like it all that much, but Captain Walker gave up his own bunk in the officers' wannigan to sleep by the door of ours. When Nialiánnguak sneaked over to our wannigan early the next mornin', she got such a fright, she woke us all up with her screamin'. It might have been funny, but all I could think of was her, the smell of her skin, the tickle of her hair. But after he sent her packin', back to the her own wannigan, Captain Walker looked on me, and said, "Carry on, soldier." He even tried to put her in another cab, with another driver the next mornin', but she put up such a fight, he had to let her ride with me, if we were ever goin' to keep to the schedule.

I dropped the diary into my lap and breathed on my fingers. My breath frosted between the fibres of my gloves, and I started to wonder if Maratse was coming back. I didn't believe it could ever happen, but what if he lost his way? What if he got disorientated in the storm? I might have died in that tunnel, too tired and too cold to get myself out. I leaned over the hole in the ice and looked down into the cavity below. The surface was black and knobbly, with less light filtering through, a dark place full of shadows. I couldn't see Serminnguaq, and I didn't want to call out for fear of forcing her deeper into the cave. At least, I thought it was a cave. From the little I could see, it brought to mind pictures I had seen in magazines of caves beneath glaciers, with rocky floors and ice ceilings, pitted with lumps of granite and other debris like a cookie dough, kept in the freezer, away from greedy fingers. Of course, now you could buy frozen cookie dough ice cream, so the analogy wasn't a good one, but it did distract me for a moment, so much so I didn't hear Arika crawling through the tunnel until she called out.

"Is that the hole?" she asked, tugging a loose strand of her hair caught in the clip of her helmet strap.

"What?" I spun around, almost guilty at the thought of being caught out, but not knowing why. "Yes," I said. "She's down there."

Arika crawled to where I sat hunched over the diary. She squeezed past me and I gave her some room to look down into the cave below. She unclipped the head torch from her helmet, leaned inside the hole, and shone it around inside. She called out to Serminnguaq but got no reply.

"We'll have to rope up before going in there," she said.

"Yes," I said, hoping she didn't mean me.

Arika crawled away from the hole and rested for a moment. She gave me a look that reeked of trouble, and I knew *I* was the one who had broken one of her laws, never mind that I was with a police officer when I did it. I was still waiting for Maratse's jurisdiction to kick in, but until then I decided to save my own skin.

"I told the Constable he would need your help," I said.

Arika dipped her head as she clipped the head torch back onto her helmet. When she looked up, I got the full treatment – the harsh tones *and* the accusatory spotlight.

"And so you should have," she said. "But now you need to get out so we can open up that hole and rope in."

I closed the diary, tucked it into my pocket along with the pencil, and crawled towards Arika. She showed no intention of moving when I reached her position, choosing to make things difficult instead.

"I agreed to you being on this expedition, because I thought you might be useful," she said.

"In what way?"

"To send a message. Your magazine – *The Narwhal* – has a pretty large readership. If you did a piece on the radioactive waste in this area, and how it's been ignored all these years, I might be tempted to put in a good word with Lærke, and let you stay on."

"And if I don't?"

"You've disobeyed my orders a couple of times now…"

I couldn't remember the second time, but let it pass as Arika moved to one side.

"…I could easily put you on the chopper when it comes to pick up Maratse."

"And Serminnguaq," I said. "I suppose she will be leaving too."

"If we can get her out. Yes, of course."

I nodded, then crawled past Arika and into the first section of the tunnel. I heard the metallic clack of karabiners and other climbing equipment being organised just outside the entrance. Maratse took my hand when I reached it, pulling me out into a whole new world, with brilliant sunshine and little more than a lick of wind to remind one were in the Arctic.

"They're going to bring her out," Maratse said. "I promised to stay here."

He tapped a cigarette out of the packet and stuck it between his lips. Maratse flicked the lighter, only to pause as one of Arika's team told him to stop.

"You don't smoke near climbing ropes," he said. "The ash can melt a spot, and you'll never know. It'll be weak then, and that day you're climbing, and it snags, that weak spot will be the death of you. Just like smoking."

I caught the look on Maratse's face and stifled a laugh. The young man could have just asked him not to smoke. Maybe he needed to explain things, taking control of at least one thing in a strange environment. It probably gave him a measure of confidence that had been shaken by the historian's death, followed by the storm. Maratse shrugged, climbed out of the trench, and chose a spot to smoke a suitable distance from the climbers as they arranged their gear. I dug the toes of my boots into the same snow steps cut into the wall of the trench and climbed up to join him.

"Serminnguaq thinks she killed Shellenberger," Maratse said. "If we're going to get her to come out of the cave, I need to tell her she didn't."

"Yes," I said.

"So, you need to read."

I opened my jacket pocket and took out the diary. The light wind curled the edges and cooled the tips of my fingers, but not enough to stop me reading.

May 5th 1960

The weather was pretty good today, but I wasn't. If it hadn't been for Nialiánnguak, I might have had it even worse. It happened in the second hour. We were drivin' at a good pace, careful, but no stops. The wind was strong, and it was playin' hell with the radios. There was some snow blowin' between the tractors, makin' it difficult to see out of the mirrors, though it was easy enough to see the tractor in front. But we were at the back. I had another attack, where I just felt like everythin' was pumpin', blood rushin' to my head, in my temples. I felt like my face would be red, if I could look at it, but I didn't want to look at it. I carried on for a bit, but then I just felt I had to stop. I took my foot off the gas, and then I just slumped over the wheel. Nialiánnguak was hollerin' but I didn't understand what she said, and I didn't much care – I felt that bad. I remember lookin' ahead, thinkin' that the tractor in front was pullin' away. I wondered why he didn't stop. But he kept gettin' further and further – at least 300 metres. That's when Nialiánnguak opened the door and jumped out of the cab, down onto the ice. She ran after the tractor, her hair blowin' sideways in the wind. That was the last I remember seein' of her – that big old jacket flappin' like a cape behind her, hair twistin', arms wavin'. When the tractor stopped, she turned and I saw her face, those big brown eyes. Even in the state I was, it was like I was lookin' through a telescope or some such. She looked so pretty, even though she looked so scared. In that moment,

*when I thought I might even die, I just thanked God that I
had met her, so pretty, so wild, so free and innocent. She
belonged on the ice and she belonged everywhere, and if
I could, I would have bought her a penthouse, draped her
in diamonds, showered her in affection. But she just stood
there, on the ice, pointin' and screamin' until Captain
Walker and a few of the men came runnin' past her. And
that was all I remembered. They told me they called in
one of the helicopters. And they told me she flew back to
the base with me. But I don't remember. I only remember
wakin' up in America. In a hospital bed, with the doctor
tellin' me he had operated on my heart, that I had a
congenital defect. But I don't know about that. My body
was in America, but my heart was back on the icecap.*

It didn't require much imagination for me to picture
Nialiánnguak waving her arms on the icecap. She could
have been right behind us, calling to us. I wondered if
Maratse thought the same thing. But, of course, we both
knew that Nialiánnguak wouldn't live longer than the
period of her pregnancy before she died in a remote
hunters' cabin, under a cold black sky. I wondered if
Frank ever knew and what he would have done if he had?

"Is there more?" Maratse asked.

I flipped through one blank page after another,
shaking my head until I came to the middle of the book.
There was a thin envelope tucked between the pages. I
opened it, carefully, pausing at a new pillow of wind
blowing up from the surface of the ice. I tucked my
fingers into the envelope when it passed and pulled out a
newspaper clipping – a thin column, folded in the middle.

"A wedding announcement," I said, peering at the
tiny print. "Frank was married in 1961." There was

another piece of paper inside the envelope, but a stronger gust of wind made pinch the envelope, stuffing it back inside the diary to protect it. I stuffed the diary back into my pocket.

"Hmm," Maratse said. He lit another cigarette.

"I suppose he never did come back for Nialiánnguak."

"They rarely do."

"What's that?"

Maratse plucked his cigarette from his lips and snubbed it out. He stuffed it back into the packet and tucked it away in the breast pocket of his jacket. He took a long breath and then sighed, kicking idly at the ice beneath his feet with the toe of his boot.

"This area," he said, with a curt nod that seemed to encompass far more than we could see, "has had a lot of visitors over the years. Explorers, geologists, traders. A lot of people. Mostly men, coming and going after a short time, especially back then."

"You mean the '60s?"

"And before." Maratse pointed in the direction of Qaanaaq, far to the north. "You can still see it in the settlements and tiny villages along the coast. History says Greenlanders needed new blood to keep the community healthy. You can believe that if you want, just like you can believe the visitors were more than happy to oblige."

I wasn't used to Maratse saying so much at one time, And so, despite the cold in my fingers and my feet, I kept still and silent.

"Anyone reading that diary," he said, "will think Nialiánnguak was a quick woman."

"*Fast*," I said, suppressing the little smile that crept onto my lips. If Maratse saw it, he didn't react.

"But they never think about life up here. You need to live life, every day, because you don't know when it's going to end. You can wait for tomorrow, but tomorrow might end with an iceberg calving, or the ice breaking, or…" Maratse shrugged. "You have to live for today," he said."Nialiánnguak lived for today."

He kicked once more at the ice, and then walked back towards the tunnel. I watched him for a moment, thinking about what he just said, thinking about Nialiánnguak, and Serminnguaq.

"Constable?" I said, jogging after him. "Arika said she'd call us when they were ready."

"Hmm," he said. "I know, but I'm not going to wait."

Part 7

There were metal ice screws along the right-hand side of the tunnel, through the hole into the low-ceilinged chamber and all the way to the cave entrance. One of Arika's young climbers worked his way along the tunnel to the exit, clipping a rope into the screws to make a handrail. It seemed excessive, but it looked safe. He crawled out of the tunnel and stood in front of it.

"Arika says you have to wear a helmet," he said, pointing at two helmets and harnesses hanging from ice axes jammed into the side of the trench. Maratse grunted and picked up a helmet. "Not so fast, she said you need to wear a harness too." The climber pointed at Maratse's utility belt, then gestured at the pistol holstered above Maratse's right hip. "You can't wear both," he said.

"*Eeqqi*," Maratse said. "I guess I can't." He stuck the helmet onto his head and pushed past the climber, ignoring his protests as he ducked inside the tunnel.

I grabbed a helmet and the two harnesses, promising to make Maratse wear one of them, "Just as soon as I catch up with him." I followed Maratse inside the tunnel, and all the way to where Arika and one of her team waited at the entrance to the cave.

"I can get you down there," she said, "but you'll need a harness."

Maratse nodded. He unbuckled his utility belt and pushed it to one side. Arika watched as I gave Maratse a climbing harness and he twisted into it.

"It's easier to rope in if you're wearing gloves." She tugged a fancy pair of leather gloves off her hands and pressed them into Maratse's. "You can wear mine."

"*Qujanaq*," he said, before clipping into the metal figure eight rappelling device Arika had prepared.

"You've done this before?"

"Once," Maratse said. "At the Academy."

"Okay," Arika said. "Hold the rope that comes out of the figure eight tight against your thigh. Lift your hand and let the rope slide through your fingers when you want to go down. Hold it tight when you want to stop. Got it?"

Maratse peered into the cave for a moment before looking at Arika. "Serminnguaq just crawled in."

"Yes, she did, but I want *you* to use a rope."

"Okay," he said. Maratse looked at me as he turned around to crawl backwards into the cave. "You're sure there's nothing more in the diary?"

"I'll look," I said, remembering the envelope.

Maratse nodded once more, then disappeared into the cave.

"Wait," Arika said. She pulled a head lamp out of her pocket, reached into the cave, and clipped it to the front of Maratse's helmet. "Shout when you need us."

The light from Maratse's head lamp flickered around the ice walls as he descended, while I opened the diary and pulled out the envelope. I let the diary sit open in my lap and placed the marriage clipping between the pages. The second piece of paper was larger and tucked inside the envelope. The fit was so tight it seemed natural to think they were original, that they were a pair. I opened the letter and turned it within the light from Arika's head lamp.

"What is it?"

"A letter from the doctor," I said.

"What about?"

"Confirming something."

It seemed that doctors of all countries shared the same need to explain things in medical terms, when layman's terms would have been far simpler. I remembered friends telling me about their conditions, only to have to find a word that I would understand in the very next sentence. I was guilty of it too, telling *my* friends I had *influenza* when I could have just told them I had a cold. There was something more dramatic and more important about a medical term, and something more sinister too.

I looked up at a shout from Maratse, that he had reached the bottom of the cave, followed by another, when he called out to say he had found Serminnguaq.

"I'm sending a harness down to you," Arika said, clipping a spare harness around the rope. "Coming now." The karabiner hummed along the rope until it clunked against Maratse's harness at the bottom.

I tapped Arika on the shoulder and asked for more light.

"It's a letter about the Schellenbergers' son," I said.

"Josh's parents?"

"Yes. Frank and a woman called Mary Jane. He must have married shortly after he got home from Greenland. They had one son," I said, turning the letter in the light. "His name was Joshua, and he had a congenital heart defect – a failure in the structure of the heart, basically a birth defect."

"So, Josh died from heart failure?"

"It seems likely," I said. "Hereditary. It says as much in his father's diary."

The letter fell into shadow, as Arika looked down into the cave. "Then why did Serminnguaq run?"

Given the time I had spent in Greenland already, I thought I had the answer. Through the many experiences I had shared with Maratse, I had learned something about shame. I understood it to be a simple emotion, a driving factor that influenced many of the terrible events that had played out in the mountains and on the ice of Greenland. Terrible because, as I understood it, it was preventable. But dealing with shame, preventing it, meant tackling it, and talking about it. Even if one could find and receive qualified help in the remote settlements and villages of Greenland, there was still no guarantee that talking about something would help. And thus, a so-called *simple* emotion, was elevated to something far more complex, just like the medical terms the doctors preferred.

But Serminnguaq had nothing to be ashamed about, or did she?

"Arika," I said. "You vetted the applications, didn't you?"

"Yes. Most of them."

"And Shellenberger's?"

"Yes, but it was Lærke who wanted him on the expedition."

"Serminnguaq didn't apply, did she?"

"No, not formally."

"She was more of an afterthought…"

"That doesn't sound very complimentary, but you could, perhaps, call her that. She was added in the comments section of the application. Shellenberger called her his *companion*."

"And Lærke said that she was approved or *overseen* because you were all busy."

"And because she was already here. That's right."

I folded the letter into the diary and crawled to the entrance of the cave, leaning out as far as Arika would let me.

"Maratse," I said.

"*Iiji?*"

"I think I have something."

Maratse shone his light up towards me. My breath caught in my throat as the light glittered within a cone of blue-veined ice, twisting up towards me, before the light collected in the pockets of dimpled ice in the walls. I peered into the light, shielding my eyes with my hand. Serminnguaq was wearing the climbing harness, and I wondered how Maratse had convinced her to put it on? I deliberated for a moment, before calling down to them both in Danish, trusting that the latest from the diary would help ease Serminnguaq's mind.

"Josh Shellenberger had a heart problem," I said, my words echoing around the glassy walls. "He was born with it. Too much exertion, like walking across the ice in cold weather – it might have caused heart failure." The light from Maratse's torch flashed to Serminnguaq's head as he looked at her. I saw a measure of relief pass across her face, lifting her long cheeks for a moment, taking some of the weight, and hopefully erasing any guilt or responsibility she might have felt over Josh Shellenberger's death. "You didn't kill him, Serminnguaq," I said. "You didn't do it."

"But that's not why she ran, is it?" Arika said.

"No," I said, sliding back a little from the entrance to

the cave. "I don't think so."

"But you have an idea?"

I did, but I wasn't sure I wanted to share it. I remembered Lærke saying she had seen Shellenberger and Serminnguaq holding hands. But she also said they often seemed to be fighting. I wondered how, if she couldn't speak English. I didn't imagine Shellenberger could speak Greenlandic, and I had not heard him speak Danish. So, unless Serminnguaq was lying about her languages, they would have been forced to communicate in other ways.

I looked up at Arika, as the sound of metal karabiners being screwed into harnesses clacked up the ice walls from the cave below.

"Imagine," I said, lowering my voice, "if a stranger came to your village."

"*My* village?"

"No, not yours. Here in Greenland."

"Okay…"

"Think about it. This man comes looking for you. He's your age. He has plenty of money – far more than you. And he says he wants to take you away with him."

"Are you asking me if I would go with him?" Arika shook her head. "Tell me this is hypothetical, before I shove your colonial arse through that hole."

"Sorry," I said, quickly, wondering if I really was cutting too fine a picture. "I mean Serminnguaq. Imagine she's twenty, and all she knows is what you've seen in the tiny settlements and villages. Then this man offers to take her away from all that."

"Where are you going with this?"

"What if she misunderstood?"

"Misunderstood?"

"She speaks no English. She's had the barest, most basic of educations, and this man whisks her away to America."

"You think Serminnguaq has been to America?"

"Josh took her," I said. "He must have."

"And?"

"And…" I let the word hang in the cold air between us, suddenly aware that I didn't want to finish that thought, not out loud. I didn't want to suggest that Serminnguaq had fallen in love with Josh, even though I was almost convinced that she had. I didn't want to say that she had misunderstood his familial longings for longings of another kind. Without an interpreter, she would never have understood the excerpt of the diary he left for her in the village below Mount Dundas, only that a man had come looking for her. A rich man. A white man. Serminnguaq was orphaned the day her mother died, and again when her grandfather died. I couldn't begin to imagine how she would feel when her companion died on the ice at her feet, perhaps in the very spot, or at least close to the place where she had been conceived. Serminnguaq's turbulent life had come full circle, and she had sought refuge from the world, deep down under the ice.

"You never finished," Arika said.

"No, I didn't."

"What were you going to say?"

"I don't think it matters," I said. "Only today matters."

Arika frowned for a second, then shook it away as she grabbed the rope. She pointed at a belay device attached to an ice screw in the wall.

"I'll need help to pull them both up."

We pulled Serminnguaq up first. I took her hand as Arika grabbed her harness. Together we pulled her out of the cave and into the tunnel. She waited, sitting quietly, one hand grasped around the handrail screwed into the ice, while we pulled Maratse out of the cave. Arika made sure that everyone was secure, before instructing us to crawl out to the surface.

I lingered for a moment, squeezing the diary in my hands, glancing at Serminnguaq, until Maratse nudged me.

"What's wrong?" he said.

"Nothing. I'm just thinking." I opened the diary, checked that the wedding clipping was tucked safely inside the pages, and then wrapped the rubber bands around the diary. I gave the envelope with the doctor's letter to Maratse. "For the medical examiner," I said.

Maratse nodded as he tucked the envelope in a pocket inside his jacket. "What about that?" he said, with a nod at the diary.

"I was thinking about leaving it here," I said, lowering my voice. "All it is is trouble." I looked at Serminnguaq as Arika helped her into the tunnel. "But it's her family history, too."

"Hmm," Maratse said. "You read it."

"Yes."

"And you have a good memory?"

"It's not bad," I said. "I *am* a writer, you know."

"*Iiji*," he said. "Then you can write it down one day, for her, for Serminnguaq. But not today," he said, as he plucked the diary from my hands. "Today is for living, and recovering, and thinking about tomorrow."

"Yes," I said, as Maratse tossed the diary into the cave. It struck me that *today* will always be more important than *yesterday*, because it is the only day you can think about *tomorrow*.

Maratse grabbed his utility belt and nodded for me to crawl on ahead of him. I followed Serminnguaq out of the tunnel and onto the icecap. I studied her face, and behind the sad eyes I saw a hidden strength, wrapped around the light that reflected from the ice. There was a second when I thought I saw something, or someone reflected in Serminnguaq's eyes. A young woman perhaps, a little wild, but full of life and energy, twirling on the ice, waving at the exciting and strange young men as they drove across the icecap to build a city of the future beneath it. They left much in their wake, much of which would take hundreds or thousands of years to clean up and eradicate. But they left life too, and today was for living.

The End

CHRISTOFFER PETERSEN

Author's Note

_____

While this novella will only give you a taste of the real story behind Camp Century, I hope it has whetted your interest to discover more. There are plenty of articles and videos on the Internet about the American secret base on the icecap, but I would also recommend the book *City under the Ice: The Story of Camp Century* by Charles Michael Daugherty, Macmillan, 1963. It reads like a wonderful bit of propaganda, but has some great details about a fascinating project.

As usual, I got a little carried away with the human aspect, and what could have occurred. When I lived in the far north of Greenland, I met people who said they could trace their genes back to some of the polar explorers who visited Greenland in the early days of exploration. It made for some interesting conversations, and, obviously, inspired this story.

However, while I have only hinted at the radioactive waste left behind as a result of the project, I do intend to return to this subject when I have more answers.

Until then, I hope you enjoyed spending an hour or so with Maratse. I certainly did.

Chris
November 2019
Denmark

CHRISTOFFER PETERSEN

Inuk

~ A short story of guilt and salvation in the Arctic ~

Inuk
human

Part 1

Police Constable David Maratse pressed the volume button on the radio until the dispatcher's voice filled the interior of the patrol car. Constable Kuno Smidt tapped the steering wheel as they waited. Three cars drove around the roundabout where *Sipisaq Kangilleq* joined the main road leading out of Nuuk city centre towards the airport and the residential area, Qinngorput. Smidt looked down at the radio as an update crackled through the speakers.

"Keep your eyes on the road," Maratse said, as he made a note of the registration number and description of the car racing out of the centre of Nuuk with two patrol cars in pursuit.

"I used to have an old Mazda, back in Denmark," Smidt said, as Maratse closed his notebook.

"When?"

"Just before I started training at the Police Academy. I sold it the night before I left for Brøndby." Smidt laughed at the thought. "Worst car I ever owned. Always breaking down."

"Hmm," Maratse said, as he scanned the cars approaching the roundabout from Nuuk.

"What about you? What car did you have?"

"I had a boat."

"Like a fishing boat?"

"Smaller," Maratse said. "And full of holes."

"Just like my Mazda."

Maratse spared a second to think about the number of cars there had been in Ittoqqortoormiit when he was old enough to drive. Apart from the police patrol car, the transit van that doubled as an ambulance, and a handful of taxis, the other vehicles were tractors and forklifts, a tanker to deliver water to those wealthy enough to afford the delivery, a flatbed truck to pick up the garbage, and a couple of vehicles to service the heliport. He couldn't remember if there had been any personal vehicles, but there were plenty of boats on the water.

"Blue Mazda," Smidt said. "There."

Maratse looked up as Smidt pointed. He saw the Mazda as the driver pulled out and around a large pick-up, accelerating down the hill to the roundabout. Maratse turned on the siren and the emergency lights, as Smidt yanked his seatbelt to take in the slack.

"This is it," Smidt said.

"Easy. Take it easy."

Smidt pulled away from the side of the road, tickling the accelerator pedal as grit spun from the back wheels of the Toyota. Despite his words of warning, Maratse grinned, helpless in the face of an imminent car chase. Most of the criminal element in Nuuk understood that it was useless to try a high-speed getaway by car – there just wasn't enough road. It was better to run on foot, or even a bicycle. The absolute best method of effecting a getaway was by boat, but it all depended upon the weather and the waves, not to mention the ice. But once in a while a younger criminal with neither the experience nor the brains to plan his getaway, chose to boost a car and race through the streets in a foolish attempt to escape and evade the police. While he would never openly admit it, Maratse secretly hoped that someone might try to run in a car each time he was stationed in Nuuk. The smile on his face said it all, as he grabbed the handrail in the side of the door and leaned back to clear Smidt's view.

"He's coming up on the roundabout," Smidt said. "I'm going to block this exit. Hold on."

Smidt stamped on the brakes as the Mazda entered the roundabout, forcing the driver to continue straight on, following the road as it curved gently upwards to the next roundabout just a few hundred metres away. Smidt waited for the two police cars pursuing the Mazda to flash past them, before speeding around the roundabout and accelerating up the hill.

The radio burst with chatter and instructions. Maratse turned it down a notch, cautioning Smidt about the next roundabout, pointing at a bus approaching from the opposite direction. Smidt nodded, gripped the wheel, and increased speed.

"Not so fast," Maratse said. "Pedestrians."

"They see us," Smidt said.

The rear lights of the Mazda and the police cars close behind it flashed red as they braked into the roundabout, one after the other, only to accelerate out of it, leaving a cloud of summer dust in their wake. Maratse pointed at the pedestrians coughing and waving their hands in front of their faces, but he didn't see the young woman on the bicycle crossing the road from the left.

Neither did Smidt.

As the front of the Toyota slammed into the woman on the bike, her body was thrown up and over the bonnet. Maratse's neck twisted, thumping in the headrest, as the woman slid over the windscreen and onto the roof, cracking the emergency light bar as she slammed into it, before dropping onto the road behind the police car. Her bicycle crunched beneath the Toyota's bumper, skewing the driver-side wheel as Smidt braked. The police car bumped into the raised centre of the roundabout and ground to a halt.

Maratse opened the passenger door and tried to leap out, only to get caught in the seatbelt. He fiddled with it for a few seconds, cursing until he managed to stab his fingers onto the button and free himself. He left Smidt, dazed but unhurt, behind the steering wheel, as he ran to where the woman lay on the road.

"Back," he shouted, waving at the pedestrians as he approached the woman. Maratse slid to his knees, resisting the urge to roll the woman onto her back so that he could see her face. Instead, he lay on the road, pressing his face close to hers, breathing a quick word of thanks as he saw the blood bubble around her mouth as she sucked in ragged lungfuls of air. Maratse pressed the transmit button on his radio and called for assistance.

Smidt joined him a few seconds later. The colour in his face evaporated with each step he took towards the woman. Maratse sent him into the road to stop traffic.

"Go," he said.

"Is she…"

"Breathing? *Iiji*. Now go."

Maratse didn't want to touch the woman, didn't want to risk causing any further injury. They had already done more than enough. But even as the flood of emotions coursed through his body, with responsibility riding on steep troughs of guilt, a sense of objectivity caught hold and forced him to observe, to see beyond the victim, the blood, and the bubbles of air on her lips.

He noticed the ear buds first – white, now bloody, but still firmly lodged inside the woman's ears. Maratse gently removed them, and then tried to talk to her. After a second or more with no response, Maratse looked around her body, saw the messenger bag that had been slung over her shoulder, but was now scuffed with a broken strap less than a metre from where she lay. He grabbed the strap and dragged the bag into his lap, unwilling to move away from the woman. Maratse dug inside the bag, found a thin wallet, and pulled out her student identity card. The card had a photo, but the young face that beamed at Maratse was unrecognisable when he compared it to the woman laying crumpled in the road. She wore her long, black hair in a ponytail in the photo, neat compared to the bloody strands stuck to her cheeks and caught in the cracks of her bicycle helmet. Maratse breathed a soft sigh of relief as he noticed the helmet, hoping that it might make a difference.

He glanced away from the woman and the card he held between his fingers, as the ambulance wailed up the hill. Smidt made a space in the traffic, urging the drivers to move their cars out of the way as the ambulance slowed to a stop a few metres from the woman.

"She went over the roof," Smidt said, as soon as the paramedics stepped out of the ambulance. "We hit her, and then she went over the roof."

"What else do we know?" said the driver of the ambulance. He walked around the woman as his partner checked her pulse.

"Her name is Mitti Petrussen," Maratse said. "She's twenty-two." He held up the card between his fingers. "She's a student at the university."

The female paramedic knelt beside Mitti, calling her name as she tried to get a response.

"Spinal board," she said to the driver. She stood as the driver jogged to the rear of the ambulance. "We'll need help to lift her."

"*Iiji*," Maratse said.

"Are either of you hurt?"

"No," Smidt said.

"Constable?" the paramedic said to Maratse. "What about you?"

"I'm fine."

"You're sure?" She looked at the two police officers, and said, "You should probably get checked out for whiplash. But let's get her into the ambulance first." She nodded at the driver, then directed Smidt and Maratse to either side of Mitti's body as she told them how and when to lift. "I've got the head," she said, as the driver pressed the spinal board to Mitti's back, and they rolled her onto it. He protected Mitti's head between blocks of foam, as the paramedic removed her hands before securing the woman's head with straps. They strapped the rest of Mitti's body, and then established an airway. The driver slid a small cylinder of oxygen between the straps and Mitti's thigh, as the paramedic slipped a mask over Mitti's mouth. "We've got her now. You can follow in your car."

"I'll stay," Smidt said. He nodded at the police car approaching from the opposite side of the roundabout. Maratse recognised it as one of the vehicles that had been involved in the pursuit. "Go with her, David. I'll sort things out here."

Maratse looked at Smidt for a second, saw a little of the colour returning to his face, and then nodded. "Meet me at the hospital," he said.

"As soon as I can."

Maratse jogged to the ambulance, pressing a hand to his neck as the driver pointed at the passenger side of the cab. He started turning the second Maratse was inside, flicking on the emergency lights and siren as he pulled away from the scene of the collision and accelerated back towards the city centre.

Maratse turned in his seat to watch as the paramedic worked on Mitti Petrussen. When the young woman's breathing changed from a gurgling rattle, to a more staccato snort, the paramedic shouted for the driver to go faster.

Despite the lack of traffic, the roads were still busy, and the drivers were not as familiar with the sight of emergency vehicles as they might have been in a larger European city. The driver cursed his way around a string of three cars before accelerating along Nuuk's main street towards *Dronning Ingrid's Hospital*.

The ambulance had barely stopped before Maratse climbed out of the passenger seat, opened the door and rushed to the rear of the ambulance. Hospital porters ordered him to stand aside as they helped the paramedic and her driver lift Mitti out of the vehicle. Maratse followed them inside, all the way to the emergency theatre before a nurse stopped him, directed him to a seat in the waiting area, with the promise to call him as soon as they knew anything.

Maratse sat down and leaned back in the chair. He closed his eyes and felt his cheeks tighten as he relived the crash, the flight of Mitti's body up and over the police car. He twitched at the swirl of blue emergency lights, screwing his eyes tight in the hope of blocking out the light.

"David?"

Maratse opened his eyes, blinking in the bright lights of the waiting room, before focusing on Constable Petra Jensen's face as she sat down beside him.

"*Piitalaat*," he whispered.

"Are you hurt?"

"*Eeqqi*, not me." Maratse nodded towards the emergency theatre.

"They've stabilised her," Petra said. "She's alive, David."

Maratse nodded as he took a long breath.

"You're sure you're all right? You look like you're in pain?"

"Not much," Maratse said. "Nothing like her."

"But still," Petra said. "You should have someone look at you." She reached out and pressed her hand over his, tugging it gently away from his neck. "You've been holding it since I got here."

"How long is that?"

Petra's lips flattened into a sad smile. "You opened your eyes the fifth time I said your name."

Maratse held Petra's hand as he rested his arm on his thigh. "We ran straight into her, *Piitalaat*."

"I know."

"She didn't stand a chance."

"She's still alive, David."

"*Iiji*," he said. "But for how long?"

Part 2

The nurse told Maratse and Petra that Mitti Petrussen was stable for the moment, but that they would know more in the morning. She said they could call for more information, but that they should give it some time.

"But there is one thing you could do," she said. "We can't find her parents in the system. We don't know who to contact – no next of kin."

"I can check," Petra said, making a note of Mitti's name and her personal identification number – her *CPR*. All Greenlanders were given one at birth, just the same as Danish children. When it came to the register of personal information, Greenlanders and Danes were equal. "You could try the Children's Home," Petra said, as she closed her notebook. "I was there until my late teens. It's worth a try."

"Yes," the nurse said. "That was our next step."

Petra waited until the nurse had left before turning to Maratse. She pressed her hand on his arm and squeezed, gently, and then harder until he looked at her.

"There's nothing more you can do," she said. "For the moment, at least."

"Hmm."

"And…" Petra paused to take a breath. "The Commissioner thinks it would be best if you and Kuno take a short leave of absence. Just until the investigation is completed." Petra turned her head towards the emergency theatre, tucking a strand of black hair behind her ear. "Once Mitti improves…"

"*If* she improves," Maratse said.

"She will. You have to believe that. And, even if you don't, you have to pretend she will, at least for the time being. Kuno is pretty shook up," Petra said.

Maratse nodded once and then stood up, stuffing his hands into his jacket pockets, then searching the chest pocket for his cigarettes. He fished the packet out of his pocket, peered inside, and then tossed the empty packet into the wastepaper bin.

"I need a smoke," he said.

"I'll come with you."

They left the waiting room and walked to the main entrance. The summer sun refused to set, casting a golden light on the windows of the high-rises that looked down on the hospital. Petra tucked her arm through Maratse's as they walked to the nearest kiosk. She waited as he bought his cigarettes, shook her head when he asked her if there was anything she wanted, and then followed him outside. Petra waited until Maratse had lit his cigarette, and then stood upwind of him, tilting her head to study his face, reaching out to take his hand.

"She's going to be okay, David."

"We hit her really hard," he said.

"But the ambulance was quick to respond. The nurse said she was stable."

Maratse sighed as he stubbed out his cigarette. "We'll see," he said, as he tossed the butt into a trash can clamped to a nearby street lamp.

"But what will you do?"

"I'm going to go home," he said.

"I can come with you. Keep you company. It's been a while since I was in Ittoqqortoormiit."

"You don't have any holiday."

"No," Petra said. "But I like the idea."

Maratse raised his thick black eyebrows – the silent Greenlandic *yes*. "I'll go hunting," he said. "Try to think a bit."

"Not too much," Petra said. She tugged her smartphone from her pocket and scrolled through her list of contacts. "I'm going to get Gaba to pick me up. Where do you want to go?"

Maratse flicked a finger towards the hospital. "I'll just look in, one more time," he said.

"They said to wait for a while…"

"*Iiji*," he said. "But, just one more time."

"You'll call me from Ittoqqortoormiit?"

"*Iiji*," Maratse said. He smiled once, and then turned to walk back to the hospital.

Petra was right; Mitti's status had not changed since they left the hospital. The nurse tried to explain to Maratse one more time, telling him that a medically induced coma was not the same as a coma, before giving up, and quietly walking back to the nurses' station in the middle of the long ward. Maratse waited by the window to Mitti's room, hands tucked into his pockets as he tried to see past the tube taped to her nose, the plastic pulsometer clamped to her finger. The machines around Mitti beeped with a regular rhythm that he could hear through the door. Maratse moved to one side as a second nurse went into Mitti's room to check her vital signs, recording them on the clipboard hanging from the bottom of the bed. She smiled at Maratse on her way out, assuring him that Mitti was not in pain, but that it would be some time before they knew anything.

"We'll keep you informed," she said.

Maratse nodded and then left the ward.

He flew the next morning, carrying little more than a toothbrush and a book stuffed into the cargo pocket of his police trousers. He landed in Kulusuk, reading and smoking while he waited for the helicopter to Ittoqqortoormiit. The summer fog was surprisingly thin, and the flights were on schedule. Maratse got a lift with the constable providing summer relief on landing in Ittoqqortoormiit. He waved his thanks once they arrived at his house, and then kicked the dust from his boots as the constable drove away. Maratse opened the door, frowned at the strips of faded red paint peeling off the frame, and went inside.

The mess in the kitchen was recent, but no worse than he remembered. Maratse ignored it. He opened the cupboards and took out a few tins, coffee, milk powder and other staples that he would need at the cabin. He collected everything into a thin plastic bag and dumped it inside the military-green backpack he found tucked behind the kitchen door. He found an empty soda bottle and slid it into one of the side pockets of the backpack, before kicking off his boots to change. He dug a pair of jeans out of the cupboard, together with a t-shirt and a thin fleece top. He dressed, tucking the fleece into the backpack together with an old sleeping bag. He pulled on his police jacket, grabbed a packet of cigarettes from the cupboard in the hall, together with a box of ammunition for the hunting rifle he kept locked in the gun closet in his room. It took almost as long to tie the laces of his hunting boots as it had to gather his things. Maratse left the house just twenty minutes after the policeman had dropped him off.

He followed the road towards the evangelical church, and then cut through the parched grass and crowberry, following a trail to the river that coursed down through the valley to the east of the village. His feet trod the familiar path, swerving gently around the known obstructions, pausing to negotiate new ones – a slip of dirt here, a slab of granite knocked by a snowmobile earlier in the year. Maratse unzipped his jacket in the heat, and adjusted the rifle slung around his chest. He stopped to smoke by the river, filled the soda bottle with glacial water, and then moved on, following the path as it narrowed, all the way to the cabin tucked into the mountainside, far enough from the village to dissuade tourists, but close enough for hunters chasing fresh sightings of reindeer.

The cabin door was open when he arrived. Maratse dumped his rifle and pack beside the door and spent the first half hour sweeping the inside and stretching his sleeping bag onto the mouse-nibbled mattress tucked against the wall of the raised sleeping platform. The cabin could sleep seven in a row at a push, but Maratse hoped he would be alone. He lit the cast iron stove, boiled water form a plastic jerry can for coffee, and then dragged one of the wooden chairs outside the cabin to sit, drink, think and smoke.

He spent the first and second cup of coffee thinking of Mitti, reliving the crash, forgetting the thrill of the chase, and focusing on the gut-punching image of Mitti lying broken in the road, blood bubbling and popping on her lips. It took two cigarettes to hear the river, and a third to see the ice on top of the surrounding mountains. A third cup of coffee helped tune Maratse into the local sounds of hares scratching in the grass behind the cabin, and perhaps – he turned slowly to look – a blue fox, padding along the tiny track to the cabin, only to abort and dart away as Maratse coughed.

But the road in Nuuk was never far away. The asphalt competed with the ice. The sirens were, at times, louder than the crash of melt water charging down the river to the fjord.

It was going to take time.

Perhaps longer than the week of leave he had been prescribed.

Maratse tossed the thoughts to one side, but they rebounded, and the asphalt returned, covering the crowberry above the river. He imagined a group of pedestrians, then one in particular – someone familiar. Maratse finished his cigarette and leaned forwards, frowning as he stared at the single pedestrian picking her way through the crowberry. She was alone. The asphalt crumbled with each step she took until Maratse could smell her, the scent of her skin – soap, earth and crowberry roots – drifting on the glacier air towards him. Her long, black hair reminded him of Petra – she looked to be about the same age, too – but there was something wilder about her. She wore a red and brown checked shirt, the tails of which flapped in the wind, tickling the sides of her threadbare jeans. Her boots were narrow, with splayed cuffs. The laces were knotted and frayed at the ends. Maratse held his breath as she approached, curious as to what she would say, and how she got here.

"You're not *Piitalaat*," he said, as he exhaled.

"I'm not," the woman said. "Were you expecting

her?"

"*Eeqqi*," Maratse said.

"But you hoped she would come?"

"*Imaqa*. Maybe."

The dirt crunched beneath the young woman's boots as she turned a slow circle to take in the cabin and the view. "It's just as I remembered," she said. "You used to run up here when you were small."

Maratse nodded.

"Usually when you had been bad," she said.

"I wasn't bad. Not all the time."

"You were cheeky. Some people said you were naughty, that you did it on purpose."

"Never on purpose," Maratse said. "Although, sometimes Tannooq told me what to do."

"*Iiji*," the woman said. "But she was punishing me."

Maratse turned his head as the woman walked past him. She peeked inside the cabin, wrinkled her nose, and said, "Something smells in here."

"The mattress," Maratse said.

"You're going to sleep on it?"

"*Iiji*."

"Rather you than me," the woman said. She brushed a sprig of crowberry off the top of a flaky barrel and sat down. "You haven't asked me yet," she said, looking at Maratse.

"I'm waiting."

"Until you're sure?"

"*Iiji*."

"I'm not real," she said. "But everything else is."

"Your shirt…"

"Is how you remember it. It was your favourite of mine. I'm wearing it for you."

"And your boots."

"Just as creased and cracked as they ever were. But comfortable. Soft. Easy to walk in." The woman smiled. "The jeans are Tannooq's. Just to annoy her."

"I know," Maratse said. "Even then, I knew."

The woman lifted her chin, turning her head slightly as the wind licked at her hair. She brushed it from her face, combing it with thin fingers, a light caramel brown, like her face, but lighter than her dark brown eyes, the same as Maratse's.

"You need to ask me," she said. "I can't help you if you don't."

"But what happens if I do?" Maratse rubbed his palm across his face. The woman smiled at the sound of his stubble scratching on his skin.

"All grown up," she said.

"*Iiji.*"

"It's okay; I won't go away, not before you're ready." She smiled again, dimpling her cheeks, encouraging Maratse until he smiled with her. "Ask me," she said.

"*Anaana*… Mother," he said.

"Yes?"

"What are you doing here?"

Part 3

Maratse blinked at the image of his mother, curious if he had drunk too much coffee, smoked too many cigarettes, or too little of both. She smiled back at him, perfectly comfortable sitting on the rusted barrel, it could just as easily have been an armchair, or her end of the sofa that she shared with his father, Umik, until a young Maratse crawled over the cushions and wormed his way onto her lap. Piipaajik had just turned fifteen when she brought Maratse into the world, and was just twenty-three when she chose to leave it.

"You haven't aged," he said, after a long period of silence.

"I died young," she said.

"You took your own life."

"*Iiji*. And you know why?"

Maratse nodded. "I'm not sure I want to talk about it," he said.

"Perhaps later?"

"*Imaqa*."

Piipaajik lifted her chin and sniffed the air as a warm breeze tousled the crowberry leaves, lifting thumbfuls of dirt from between the hardy and gnarled roots, before splashing it against their boots, into the cotton pores of their jeans, and, finally, against the sides of the cabin.

CONSTABLE DAVID MARATSE #3

"There are other things to talk about," Piipaajik said. "More important things."

"Like what?" Maratse asked.

"Miliisa."

Maratse turned the cup in his hand. He shook his head, and said, "Her name is Mitti."

"The woman in the hospital?"

"*Iiji.*"

"I know her name," Piipaajik said. "But I think you need to talk about Miliisa before you're ready to help the young woman."

"Before I'm *ready*? They said there was no news. They said it would take time."

"Hmm," Piipaajik said, softer than Maratse ever did, but loud enough to capture his attention. Her lips creased as she smiled at the frown on his face. "Isn't that what you would say? Or should I add a little more *unh*?" she said, adding a sneer to her lips, if only for a second before she started to laugh.

"You came to mock me," Maratse said. "I understand now."

"No, not to mock you, but to help you understand. Mostly because you don't. Not yet. Not until you talk about Miliisa."

"*Mitti.* Not *Miliisa.*"

Maratse tipped the last dregs of coffee into the dust at his feet and stood up. He looked at his mother, curious that he had brought her with him, anxious too as to what it might mean. Regardless of what Piipaajik wanted him to understand, he understood that before he could send his mother away, he must process the collision and systematically work through the details and the emotions he had attached to each of them. But no matter how insistent she was – or how insistent *he* was – Maratse struggled to make the connection between the young woman lying in hospital and a five-year-old girl from his childhood called Miliisa. He left his mother sitting on the barrel, ducked his head, and went inside the cabin. Piipaajik was standing beside the wood-burning stove when he lifted his head.

"You have to talk about her," she said. "I won't go before you do."

"Perhaps I want you to stay? If I don't mention her…"

"You will get tired of my company," Piipaajik said. "And you still won't be able to help the girl."

"Mitti?"

"Yes."

Maratse said nothing more for the next few minutes. He took the cans of food, coffee and the powdered milk from his backpack. He found a place for all of it on the thin, rickety table that doubled as a kitchen counter, larder and desk. Piipaajik followed him around the cabin, giving him a start each time he forgot about her – she made no footfalls, cast no shadows. But she was there every time he looked. Her cheeks and the dimples of her smile, softened the strong lines of her jaw and her determined chin that lifted each time she tried to catch his attention

"You can't ignore me, Qilingatsaq," she said, calling Maratse by his given name – the one *she* gave him. "I won't let you."

"It's *me* that won't let me," he said, shaking his head at the absurdity of it all. "Maybe I just need to rest?"

"I'll be here when you wake."

"I'll sleep late."

"Like you did as a boy?"

"*Iiji*," he said. "Just like that."

He pictured his bedroom, the single mattress on the hardwood floor; it was only slightly narrower than his parents' in the room next door. But where he slept was never important, it was where he *played* and explored that the young Maratse lived for. The river – *this* river – was where he scrambled as a child, crawling over and around the boulders, stopping to scratch at the crunchy black lichen that stuck to his palms. He remembered someone calling his name one day as he picked at the lichen, holding his hand in front of his face, biting his bottom lip in concentration. He was five – if he remembered right. A tangle of black hair, curled in places, sticking upright in others. The five-year-old Maratse had no qualms about running around in over-sized rubber boots, bare knees and grubby underpants, with a t-shirt two sizes too big flapping in the wind as he ran.

Someone called his name again – turning his five-year-old head. And then Maratse could see her, Tannooq, his mother's sister. She was fifteen when he was five, the spitting image of Piipaajik, but for the jealous scowl that twisted her young face. Maratse knew that look as a child, and he remembered it as an adult – it was his fault she had lost the attention of his sister. But through him, and the wild schemes she whispered into his head, she would have her revenge.

"But not that day," Maratse said, as he picked up the tin of ravioli, turning it in his hands as he searched the windowsills for a tin opener.

"You're remembering," Piipaajik said.

"I'm looking for something to open this with," he said, holding up the can.

"No," she said. "You were down by the river. Tannooq was calling to you."

"Like she did most days."

"But this wasn't most days, Qilingatsaq. You remember, don't you?" Piipaajik walked across the cabin floor. She stopped beside Maratse, pressed her hand over his.

"You're cold," he said.

"Never mind about that. Miliisa," she said. "Think about her."

"I need to open this can. I need to eat."

"*Eeqqi*," Piipaajik said. She slapped at Maratse's hand. "This is important. What did Tannooq want? Think!"

Maratse put the can down on the windowsill and went outside. Piipaajik followed him, calling his name as he followed a familiar track down to the river.

"Is this the rock?" she asked, when Maratse paused beside a boulder. "Are these your palm prints?" She traced two small patches of stubbly lichen between the clumps of crispy black leaves.

"Not my prints," he said, walking on to the river.

Maratse stopped at the water's edge. It was brown with silt. He knew it would settle if one left it for long enough. He should have brought a can, or a bucket.

"Did you come here, first?" Piipaajik asked. "To the water? Where did you go next?"

Maratse turned as the stones crunched beneath Piipaajik's feet. He frowned at the sound, curious that she could make it, that he was *conjuring* it. He looked at her face, smiled as he realised that she looked exactly as she did before she died. A closer look revealed a thin scar around her neck. It was thick in places. Piipaajik saw where he was looking and fiddled with her collar to hide her neck.

"This isn't about me," she said.

"Why not?"

Piipaajik shook her head. "Stop changing the subject."

"Hmm," he said, louder and deeper than she had.

"You came to the river. You wanted to cross it. But the water flowed too fast." Piipaajik pointed at the torrent of brown water surging across the flat rocks, crashing and splashing against the boulders. "Tannooq told you to cross."

"That's not what happened," he said. "She saved me, *anaana*. Or don't you want to hear that?"

"This isn't about me. Stop changing the subject."

Maratse looked at the river; he remembered the water pressing against the toes of his rubber boots, then the sides as he took another step into the river. It was cold, colder even than the sea. He remembered looking over his shoulder at Tannooq. She wore the scowl that he learned would often get him into trouble, so he took another step into the river, lifting one foot, despite Tannooq yelling and screaming for him to stop. He raised his short leg, bent his tiny knee, and aimed for the flat boulder just in front of him – not far at all, but too far for a five-year-old boy in yellow y-fronts and a faded blue cotton t-shirt.

If Tannooq hadn't been there.

If Tannooq hadn't run down to the river.

"You would have drowned," Piipaajik said. "But you didn't."

"I didn't."

"What happened next?"

"She grabbed my arm, pulled me out of the water," Maratse said. "I lost my boots."

"And she carried you home?"

Maratse sighed. "You know she didn't."

"I know she didn't," Piipaajik said. "Tell the story, Qilingatsaq. Tell all of it."

Maratse turned away from the river. He brushed past his mother as he walked along the narrow track back towards the cabin. He walked past it, stopping only when they could see the first houses, distant but easily recognisable.

"That one," he said. "The first one. She took me there."

"You were wet."

"And shivering. I was hypothermic."

"You needed help," Piipaajik said.

"She had no choice." Maratse waited for Piipaajik to nod, reaching out for her when she didn't. "*Anaana*," he said. "She had to take me there. It was the very first house."

"I know."

"Then forgive her," Maratse said. "At least forgive her for that, if not for the other thing." Maratse waited for his mother to nod, and said, "*You* wanted me to tell this story."

"Because it will help."

"I still don't see how," he said.

"We'll come to that." Piipaajik smiled. "What happened next?"

"He was home, of course."

"That's right. He always was. She should have known that. Tannooq should never have taken you there."

"*Anaana*?"

Piipaajik crossed her arms over her chest and nodded. "Sorry. Go on," she said.

"Angiseq was in the kitchen," Maratse said.

He remembered the kitchen. One of the windows was missing, covered with a patch of carpet and sealed with cloth tape. The sun shone through the fibres – strong in some places, weaker in others, but enough to light Angiseq's face, the black frost burn on his cheek from the previous winter, and the splashes of beer on his chin from the bottle in his hand. There was little else in the kitchen, and what little there was could not be used. Broken plates were stacked on warped counters, cracked mugs on slanted shelves.

"There were flowers in one of the mugs," Maratse said. "I think she must have picked them."

"Who did?" Piipaajik asked. "Who picked the flowers?"

Maratse shook his head. "It's not important."

"It is."

"It might not have even been her."

"It was. Who else?"

Maratse pointed at the house in the distance. He stepped to one side, as if to give his mother a better view. The flat of his hand marked the outer wall.

"He told Tannooq to put me on the bed, beneath the blankets," Maratse said. "In the room to the right of the kitchen."

"And she did."

"*Iiji.*"

"But there was someone else in the bed, wasn't there?"

"*Iiji.*"

"You knew her?"

Maratse nodded.

"But you didn't talk to her. Not at first."

"I was shivering," Maratse said. "She was crying."

"Quietly," Piipaajik said. "You told me she was crying quietly."

"*Iiji.*"

Maratse scratched at his nose. He brushed at an imaginary fly – no less real than his imaginary mother. The thought made him smile, but it faded from his lips when Piipaajik spoke.

"You said she held your hand. You said she lay close to you, that the warmth of her body made you warm. That you stopped shivering."

"I don't remember."

"Yes," Piipaajik said. "You do remember. Because she told you what he did to her. She whispered it, and then you told me."

"Tannooq took me there to save me. She had to."

Piipaajik walked to Maratse's side. She curled her arm around his waist and pressed her head against his shoulder. "I know."

"What I did next," Maratse said. "I had to do that too."

"I know."

"It wasn't Tannooq's fault. And it wasn't the girl's either. But she paid for it," he said.

"It will help if you say her name."

Maratse cleared his throat. He swallowed once before he said, "Miliisa. That was her name."

Part 4

The cabin door creaked on rusted hinges, flaked with bright orange and brown. Maratse pushed at the door from inside the cabin, pressing it into the frame as the wind picked up outside, blowing dust onto the toes of his boots.

"I don't want to talk about what happened next," he said.

"Then why did you come?"

"I was sent away."

"You were given leave, Qilingatsaq," Piipaajik said. "It's not the same thing. You could have stayed in Nuuk, but you chose to come here."

"This is my home."

"It's where you have a house. It's not your home."

"But this cabin…"

The last words of the sentence, whatever it might have been, died on his lips. Maratse pressed his forehead against the door, felt the striations of rough wood tickle his skin, smelled the dry scent of wind-leached timbers and fat – fat from cooking, fat from butter, reindeer fat.

"I came to hunt," he said. "I came for the reindeer."

"They're not here, Qilingatsaq. Not now."

"I know," he whispered.

"Then why did you come?"

Maratse turned his head, then his body. He leaned back against the door, felt the soft thumps of wind fists, heard the knocking, the insistent pledge to disturb long into the light night when the sun didn't dip, and the image of his mother would not fade.

"Not until you answer the question, at least," she said.

The tin of ravioli was on the windowsill where he left it. Maratse spotted the dull edge of the opener lying in the dust beside it. He shook his head – it had been there all along. Maratse pierced the lid in two places and placed the can on top of the stove. He added more wood and made a mental note that he should walk into town before he had to leave to replace the fuel he had used. Cabins in Greenland could prolong lives. Well-stocked cabins could save them. The tomato sauce sputtered as the can warmed. Brown bubbles blistered and popped around the holes Maratse had pierced in the lid.

"Qilingatsaq…" Piipaajik said, her voice soft, almost hidden by the bubble and spit of Maratse's dinner.

"*Iiji.*"

"Miliisa," she prompted.

"She held my hand," he said. "She kept me warm."

"And?"

"She told me that Angiseq, her father, had beaten her." Maratse used a rag from the table to lift the can from the stove. He put it on the floor to cool. "He was drunk, she said."

"But he didn't just beat her."

"*Eeqqi,*" Maratse said, quietly. He sighed. "No, he didn't."

"When you came home that night, you couldn't look at your father."

"*Ataata* never touched me."

"I know, but you couldn't look at him. You couldn't look at any man for a week."

"She held my hand so tight," Maratse whispered.

"I remember. You told me." Piipaajik sat down on the sleeping platform, resting her elbows on her thighs, curling her fingers over her knees. "I watched you for a whole day, never letting you out of my sight. I remember you had this kind of shake, like a tremor through your little body. You couldn't control it."

"I remember," Maratse said.

"You *are* remembering," she said. "You brought me here. I am you."

"I know," he said. "But…"

"You don't want to be alone?"

"That's right."

Piipaajik lifted her chin and looked at Maratse. He crouched in front of the stove, gripped the tin and levered the opener into the holes in the lid until he could peel it off. Piipaajik laughed when he grumbled that he had no spoon.

"You could be more useful," he said.

"Try the cupboard."

Maratse left the tin to cool and opened the medicine cupboard hanging on the wall. The door creaked and dropped off the bottom hinge as he opened it. There was a plastic spatula inside, the kind one might use to smooth resin on a boat. Maratse cleaned it on his elbow and then lifted the cupboard door into place. He remembered something else about the cupboard, but pushed the thought to one side. Piipaajik talked while he ate.

"I was angry at Tannooq. I told her you were scared of Angiseq, and that you hadn't slept all night."

"I didn't," Maratse said. He licked at the tomato sauce, and then wiped his chin with the back of his hand. "But you shouldn't be angry at Tannooq. About the other thing, yes, but not that."

"She chased you into the river," Piipaajik said.

"She carried me back to the village." Maratse looked at the young version of his mother. It was the last version – she would die two years later, when he was just eight years old. "We don't have to agree on this," he said.

"We never will."

Maratse shrugged. He ate the rest of the ravioli, quietly impressed at the way the spatula flexed around the insides of the tin to capture all but the most stubborn and burnt patches of pasta and sauce. He washed his meal down with the last of the water from the soda bottle, and then boiled the remaining water in the pan for another cup of coffee. The water bubbled and steamed as Piipaajik continued.

"I knew you were going to do something," she said. "You had that look. It was a new look – new for you. But your father had it too, when he was determined to do something. But when he wore the look it was out of stubbornness, yours was more a look of righteousness, like you were going to put things right." Piipaajik pointed at Maratse and smiled. "Now you have the jacket to go with it."

"I didn't know what would happen," Maratse said.

"How could you? You were five?"

"He didn't have to do it."

"I don't think he knew what he was doing," Piipaajik said. She paused for a moment, and then added, "It doesn't make it better."

"Nothing will."

"But you still think you're responsible, don't you?"

"*Iiji*," Maratse said. He waved his hand for Piipaajik to continue. "We've begun. Let's continue."

"You're ready now?"

"*Iiji.*"

"And you'll admit that's why you came here?"

"Yes.

"Say it."

Maratse grunted something under his breath, and then lifted his head as Piipaajik reached out to press her fingers under his chin.

"I came here because this is where it happened, the first time."

"Go on."

"The first time I was responsible, that what I did…"

"Yes?"

"Ended badly," he said, glancing into a dusty corner of the cabin.

Piipaajik pulled back her arm, and said, "That's a start, but you can do better than that."

"I know," Maratse said.

He spent the next few minutes fiddling with the water, the pan, the instant coffee. He let it cool as he walked down to the river to collect more water. The wind blew grit into his eyes, he screwed them shut. The silt swirled within the pan, he let it settle. Piipaajik sat outside the cabin, wind tugging at her wild hair. Maratse tucked the pan inside the cabin, brought out his coffee and joined her. It was Maratse's turn to sit on the barrel, while Piipaajik leaned back in the chair. He smoked once he was finished with his coffee, curious at how his mother waved her hand at the smoke in her face, caught by the wind, dragged out of Maratse's lungs.

"I never smoked," she said. "I don't know why you have to."

Maratse shrugged. "I'm nearly finished."

"Finish now and we can finish this."

Maratse said nothing. He took another drag on his cigarette, wondering if he smoked one more that his mother might stay a little longer. He had missed her, could still feel the emptiness of his sour stomach, the rawness of his throat, the sting of his tears on his cheeks.

"But that was her death," he whispered. "We were talking about another."

"One death at a time, Qilingatsaq."

"*Iiji.*"

Maratse finished his cigarette. He stuffed the butt into the packet, tucking it inside his jacket pocket. He spent another few minutes watching the wind tease out the full length of Piipaajik's hair, only to twist it back again, curling it around her face so that she had to brush it from her eyes to look at him.

"You're stalling," she said.

"I know."

"Do you want me to carry on?"

Maratse raised his eyebrows – *yes*.

"Okay," she said. "You were helping *ata*, your grandfather, when it happened. I sent you over to the drying racks so that he could keep an eye on you. You were bashing teeth from the halibut heads."

"I remember."

"You cut your knuckles."

"*Iiji.*"

"And he sat you on his lap to look at them. You asked if you could see his knife – the one he wore on his belt."

"It was a cheap one," Maratse said. "The blade was rusty…"

"And the handle was melted on one side." Piipaajik laughed. "You talked about it all the time. You thought it was the most exciting thing in the village. You thought it was expensive, priceless."

"Not priceless," he said. "It had a price."

"Yes," Piipaajik said. She waited until Maratse nodded that he was ready. "Angiseq came down the hill towards the drying racks."

"I watched him all the way."

"*Ata* thought you were ill. He said you looked so pale, and that you were holding your breath."

"And the knife," Maratse said.

"You slipped off his lap."

"With the knife."

"*Ata* said you started to scream. I think I heard you. I would recognise your scream from a thousand screams, but I couldn't have stopped you even if I had tried. Even if I had been there."

"No one could," Maratse said. "*Ata* was there. He couldn't stop me."

Piipaajik told the story, but Maratse stopped listening. His mother's words whirled around him in the wind. He felt the tickle of her hair on his cheek, but it could just as easily have been fishing line, the ends of lines stretched out to be mended. They had slowed him down as he ran. He had to kick free of them. But he did, and he screamed with every step. He remembered Angiseq's face, the expression of shock that twisted through his beer-slack features, then the recognition, the boy, Maratse, the knife in his hand, the tip of it coming closer and closer as the boy ran towards him.

"Not *towards* him," Maratse said, interrupting his mother. "I was running *at* him."

"It's your story," she said. "You tell it."

Maratse took a long breath, and then said, "I ran at him. The rubber boots – the ones Tannooq had rescued from the river – were still wet." Maratse wriggled his toes inside his hunting boots, as if his socks were wet from the river. "I clumped more than I ran. It was almost funny."

"No-one was laughing."

"*Ata* was shouting," Maratse said. "He shouted for me to stop, to put the knife down before I hurt myself. But he didn't know that I wasn't going to hurt myself, I was going to hurt him. I was going to kill Angiseq, for what he did to his daughter, for what he did to Miliisa."

"But you didn't kill him, Qilingatsaq."

"I should have."

"But you didn't."

Maratse remembered stumbling as the tip of his grandfather's knife pierced Angiseq's jeans and then further, deeper into his thigh. There had been a lot of blood, and then more as the five-year-old Maratse had gripped the handle of the knife, ratcheting it up and down, too weak to pull it out, still screaming – too loud to hear Angiseq cursing and shouting at him. He didn't feel Angiseq's first strike – the clap hand that made his ear swell. But he felt the second, felt the man's rough hands grip his tiny chin, lifting Maratse off the ground, tugging him away from the knife, before he slapped him once more, and then tossed him into the dirt and gravel at his feet.

"Your grandfather picked you up," Piipaajik said. "I saw him do it. And I saw Angiseq covered in blood, and your bloody hands. I saw your grandfather's knife in

Angiseq's thigh. It was still there when the policeman came."

"I don't remember the policeman," Maratse said.

"You screamed until your throat was dry. I tried to give you some water, but you pushed me away. I had to hold you for the rest of the night – too frightened to let go. I thought you would go after Angiseq again. I thought you would try and kill him."

"I should have," Maratse said. "I should have tried."

"But you didn't," Piipaajik said, taming her hair with one hand, as she stood up to press her hand against Maratse's cheek. "You didn't."

"No, but he did."

Part 5

Hunters' cabins in Greenland come in all shapes and sizes. Built from pallets taken from the docks, built with panels from houses destroyed in piteraq winds, built with windows – or not, built with care – or not, but above all built to last until the snow, the wind, or the bear breaks them down. The sun plays its part too, bleaching the timbers, stripping the paint, expanding the walls and the doors, the window frames, even the roofs, with persistent summer-long sun. Until the winter takes over, with its wood-shrinking temperatures, the expansion of ice in the cracks, the weight of snow on the roof, and the hungry bear.

Despite the destructive forces of the Arctic, its preservative powers are equally strong. Dead organic matter, both human and beast, desiccates, dries up once the initial bloat has run its course. It's not unusual to find reindeer or musk ox skeletons draped with hairy hides, a refuge for lemmings in the winter perhaps. There's a reason that scientists search for mammoths in the Arctic, searching for whole strings of DNA.

But the Arctic preserves other things too, and the cabin is no exception. Neither is it exceptional. Is it not often the way that the abandoned barn in the far field, or the railway siding in a derelict yard, or even the empty house on the corner of a quiet neighbourhood attracts evil people, providing refuge for evil deeds?

The barrel dimpled with a dull popping sound as Maratse stood up. He looked at the door, curious to note the wind tugging at the latch – a polar bear handle that had to be turned upwards to open.

"It happened here," Piipaajik said. "Didn't it?"

"You know it did. We both do. We both came here."

"You came before me."

"*Iiji*," he said, as he remembered worming free of his mother's arms and running out of the house as she slept.

The late summer light cast shadows as the sun spun a long slow circle in the sky. The young Maratse, wearing just a t-shirt and grubby jogging trousers, dirty sneakers on his feet, ran up the road towards Miliisa's house. He slowed at the door, heart thumping in his small chest, small fingers clenched in small fists. The door was open, and he stepped inside, spurred on by Miliisa's words, her description of the things her father did when he was drunk.

"I think he's sick," she had said. "Maybe he can't help it?"

"*Imaqa*," Maratse had said, unsure of what else he could say. Some of the things that adults did required an adult vocabulary to put them into words. He didn't have one yet, but he could *sense* things. He understood when things were not right.

Was it right to stab Angiseq in the thigh? Was it right to try and kill him?

The young Maratse had *sensed* that it was, and it was up to his older self to make adult sense of it, to speak of things with his adult words.

"Miliisa?"

The walls gobbled up Maratse's small voice, just as the silence inside Miliisa's house threatened to swallow his five-year-old courage. He backtracked to the door, onto the gravel street, and then further up the track towards the cabin in the valley.

"I ran all the way," Maratse said, turning his head to look at Piipaajik. "But I was too slow." He turned the door handle and opened the cabin door, stepping inside as soon as Piipaajik nodded that she was ready.

No matter what had occurred inside a remote cabin, the need for shelter often overruled any concerns or qualms one had about spending the night. The cabin was more robust than most. It had seen many winters – seen them and shrugged them off. The interior showed more signs of wear than the walls or the roof. Even the chimney had fared better than the cupboards. It was often the case that humans cared less for something after it was built than during the time it had taken to build it. A disproportionate allocation of care and attention, but it was also easily understood that the outer walls and the roof mattered far more than the cupboards or furniture inside. One could live without them or even burn them in the coldest of winters. Such practicality, commonplace in the Arctic, allowed one, in times of need, to overcome emotional restraints and limitations. It was Arctic practicality that allowed Maratse to stay at the cabin, together with a need to explore his memory of the place, to dig deep, down where it hurts.

"One death at a time, Qilingatsaq," Piipaajik said. She followed him inside.

"That's where she was," Maratse said, pointing at the corner of the cabin to the left of the door. "I saw her when I came in," he said.

"That wasn't all you saw."

Maratse looked into the corner, remembering Miliisa's pale cheeks, her blue lips, the strange angle of her right leg, her small hands – open, fingers flat. He kept looking at the corner, but pointed to his right, towards the cupboard clinging to the wall.

"Angiseq was there," he said. "There was a rope around the cupboard – old fishing line. It caught in the cupboard door."

"Nearly pulled it off," Piipaajik said.

Maratse nodded. "Nearly." He turned away from the spot where Miliisa's father had strangled her, turned to look at the opposite corner of the room where Angiseq had hung himself. "Miliisa said she thought her father was sick," he said. "But he wasn't too sick for remorse, or guilt." Maratse took a long, slow breath. "I felt guilty."

"You still do," Piipaajik said.

Maratse turned to look at her. "I thought we said *one death at a time*?"

"They're related," she said. "You know that."

"Guilt," Maratse said.

"Yes." Piipaajik walked to the corner where Miliisa had died. "You feel guilty about her death. You think you're responsible."

"I was. I attacked her father. He knew why and he killed her for it."

"You were five years old," Piipaajik said.

"That's what the adults said. I didn't understand them. I didn't have the words."

"The adults." Piipaajik sighed as she sat down on the edge of the sleeping platform. "I was barely an adult then. I was still a child when I had you. But I knew enough to know that you couldn't be responsible for what happened then, and you can't now."

"Mitti?" Maratse said.

"That's why you came here, isn't it?"

"I don't know," he said. "*Imaqa.*"

"More than *maybe*," Piipaajik said. "You came here because you feel responsible for what happened to the young woman in Nuuk. You think it's your fault." Piipaajik shook her head as Maratse started to speak. "This is why you brought me here, so don't interrupt."

"Okay," he said.

"You're used to responding to other people's pain, to solving other people's problems. That's your job. You trained for it, and you're good at it. It's okay to say that, to admit that, even though you wouldn't say it to anyone else. Never."

"I don't talk about things like that."

"No, you don't. Perhaps you should."

"Who would listen?"

"Petra would," Piipaajik said.

"*Piitalaat.*" Maratse nodded. He looked in the pan to see if the silt had settled enough to decant the surface for coffee.

"It's not ready yet," Piipaajik said. "Stop looking for distractions." She waited for Maratse to look at her before continuing. "You deal with other people's problems, often the things they are responsible for. You have felt responsible for two things in your life. Miliisa's death," she said, pointing at the dusty corner of the cabin. "And now Mitti. But she's not dead, Qilingatsaq. And you're wasting time."

"How?"

"You came all this way, when you know you should be somewhere else."

"I was told to take a leave of absence."

"And you chose to leave." Piipaajik laughed. "You're stubborn for a reason," she said. "And when you find a reason to be stubborn, you usually choose to ignore what you're told to do. Only this time it was different. Because you feel responsible."

"I am."

"You feel guilty."

"I do."

"And when have you ever let such thoughts influence your actions?"

"I did then," Maratse said, nodding at the corner of the cabin. He caught another mental glimpse of Miliisa's body, before Piipaajik's words pushed the dead girl out of his mind.

"You were five, Qilingatsaq. It's time to grow up."

Piipaajik stood up and walked across the cabin to the door. She opened it and stepped outside, pausing for a moment as the wind caught her hair, before turning to follow the path back to Ittoqqortoormiit.

"Where are you going?" Maratse said, raising his voice as Piipaajik walked into the wind. "You can't leave." He grabbed his rifle and slung it over his shoulder. He stuffed the sleeping bag inside his backpack, and hurried out of the cabin. He stopped at the door when he remembered the stove. The ashes were still warm. He closed the glass door of the stove, and then the door of the cabin as soon as he was outside.

Maratse tugged the backpack onto his shoulder and marched after Piipaajik. There was an urgency about her. She walked with long strides, the tails of her shirt flapping at her sides, twisting back and forth as she moved her arms to the rhythm of her march.

"*Anaana*," Maratse said, hurrying to catch her. "Where are you going?"

"Where are *we* going?" she said, brushing her hair from her face as Maratse fell into step beside her. "You're the one who determines where we go. Where do *you* want us to go?"

"The graveyard," he said. "It's time for the next death."

"Both of them," Piipaajik said.

She said nothing more until they reached the dusty outskirts of the village. Maratse caught himself glancing at the people on the roads, wondering if they could see her too, knowing that they couldn't. Some of the older residents might remember her, but no-one could see her. Maratse followed Piipaajik to the graveyard, dumped his backpack by the side of the road, and followed her to the graves. Thin white crosses, bright like the icebergs in the bay, stood proud of the granite, grit and grasses covering the graveyard. Piipaajik led Maratse to two crosses. Her name was carved into one of them, the name of her sister, Tannooq, was carved into the other.

"I never forgave her," Piipaajik said. "For what she did."

The wind tugged at her hair as she reached for Maratse's hand.

"*Anaana*," he whispered. "I don't know if it is me or you talking right now."

"Does it matter?"

"It matters, because I forgive her." He squeezed her hand, curious that he could, wondering what it meant. "Tannooq loved you," he said. "She missed you from the moment I was born and was jealous of me from the moment you knew you were pregnant."

"It wasn't your fault."

"*That* is something I have never doubted," Maratse said, allowing himself a thin smile. "And it's why I can forgive her, and you can't."

Piipaajik turned to face Maratse. She gripped his hands. "I don't regret having you, Qilingatsaq. Never."

"I know," he said. "But you were too young. And Tannooq loved you. She wasn't ready for you to be a mother. She wasn't ready to lose her sister. Neither of you were. So," he said, with a nod to Tannooq's grave. "You have to forgive her."

"She slept with your father."

"I know."

"To punish me."

"*Iiji*," Maratse said. "And then you punished all of us, when you took your own life." Piipaajik scowled as she tried to pull away. Maratse held on. "Not yet. I'm not ready to let go of you just yet."

Piipaajik looked past Maratse's shoulder, and said, "There are children on the road. They will hear you talking to yourself. They'll think you're crazy."

"No distractions," Maratse said. He held Piipaajik by the shoulders, turning her to face the graves, Tannooq's and her own. "She has suffered enough," he said. "Go and find her. Be with her now."

"You need me."

"*Eeqqi*," he said, with a gentle shake of his head. "I did need you; I will always miss you, but now I have to let you go." He looked over his shoulder and waved at the children. "They do think I'm crazy," he said.

Piipaajik was gone when he turned his head. Maratse frowned at her sudden disappearance, and then laughed at the thought. He lit a cigarette, rolled it into the gap between his teeth, and stuffed his hands into his jacket pockets. The women in his family had lived too fast, burning brightly at the very edge of the world. He could feel the heat. It had fuelled his journey to Ittoqqortoormiit, to the cabin, it had sustained him through his memory of Miliisa's murder, and it would drive him onwards, back to Nuuk, back to the young woman who lived, who he should never have abandoned.

"I'll be stubborn, *anaana*," he said. "I promise."

Part 6

Maratse landed in Nuuk after a delay of several hours at the airport on the island of Kulusuk. The fog gave him time to think, to wonder at his projection of Piipaajik, and to smile, privately, at the time spent with his mother. Perhaps the details had been a little off, her hair longer than he remembered, her shirt softer than the one she wore on the day she took her own life. But he could forgive such minor discrepancies. He was learning to forgive a lot, or at least to ease up on his sense of responsibility, and his role in certain events. However he decided to interpret the past – with or without his mother's help – nothing could change the fact that a series of events led to Miliisa's death. Maratse was neither more nor less responsible for what happened, but he had played a part, regardless of the role.

The same could be said of his role in the collision – the team leading the inquiry wouldn't call it an accident before all the evidence had been collected and processed. He had played his part, but he was not done, not yet. But for one of the few times in Maratse's life, he felt a stab of impatience when he looked at the fog. He needed to be in Nuuk, but the blanket of impenetrable grey cloud draped over the airport disagreed.

He would wait, as he always did.

Petra met him at the airport in Nuuk. She waved from the driver's seat of the dark blue Toyota, before opening the door and walking across the parking area to greet him.

"They said you were coming back early," she said. "I thought you could use a lift."

"*Iiji*," he said, before pausing to smile. "It's good to see you, *Piitalaat*."

"It's good to be seen," she said.

Maratse frowned at the curious curl of her lips and the spark of something he could not define in her eye. Had he been younger, or if such things mattered, he might have looked for something in her smile, but when he wasn't working it was the land, the sea and the ice that called to him. He didn't have time for anything else.

Petra, for her part, enjoyed the slight confusion she caused Maratse, and saved such smiles for him, knowing that she didn't care that he was older, and that she would wait for the time when he no longer felt the same pull of the ice, or when the appeal of something else was stronger.

"I can wait," she said, confusing him further.

"What for?"

"You haven't told me where you want to go." Petra hiked her thumb over her shoulder at the patrol car. "I came to give you a lift. Remember?"

"*Iiji*," he said. "I want to go to the hospital."

"She's still in a coma," Petra said. "But we can go. And then I need to take you somewhere." Petra curled her arm around Maratse's and tugged him towards the car. "You look like you found some answers," she said, "and I want to hear about it. But once we're done at the hospital, you need to talk to Kuno." She let go of Maratse as they reached the car. "He's taking it very hard."

Maratse nodded, opened the car door and sat down in the passenger seat. He had to blink for a moment, re-framing the familiar dashboard, radio, and interior from the moment when Mitti Petrussen rolled up and over the bonnet, to the present time, in the car park at Nuuk airport.

"Are you okay?" Petra asked.

"*Iiji*." Maratse buckled his seatbelt and closed the door. "It's the same car."

"It's the same type," Petra said, as she started the engine.

Petra pulled out of the parking spot and accelerated away from the airport. She said nothing for the first few minutes, but as they approached the roundabout where Mitti had crashed into the police car, Petra brought Maratse up to speed on what she had discovered in the short time Maratse had been on the east coast.

"She is an orphan," she said. "But she wasn't at the children's home in Nuuk. It was Maniitsoq." Petra slowed at the roundabout, sparing a glance at Maratse before she continued. "Her parents died in a house fire when she was six. The council couldn't find a suitable family member to take her, so they put her in the children's home." She paused and forced a smile when Maratse looked at her. "It's a familiar story, don't you think?"

Maratse nodded as he remembered that Petra had spent her childhood in a similar home. He liked to think of her being one of the success stories, leaving the home in her late teens, and forging a career in the police. But she rarely talked about it, often saying that *there wasn't much to tell*, or similar excuses. It seemed that everyone in Greenland had something they didn't want to talk about. And, if they did, it often turned out they were hiding something else, deeper, inaccessible.

"Hmm," Maratse said, nodding when Petra said they should probably wait until the official visiting hours, and that they had time to drive down to the water.

She parked close to the old hospital, zipping her jacket all the way up to the top of the collar as she stepped out of the car. She nodded at the bench beside the wooden rack of traditional *qajaq*s and sat down as Maratse lit a cigarette. Petra sat quietly for a few minutes, staring at the stone effigy of Sedna, and at the chunks of ice rolling in the black water around the animals engraved into the base of the sculpture. Maratse extinguished his cigarette with a pinch of his fingers and tucked the last half into the packet. He sat down, stuffed his hands into his pockets and stared out to sea.

"You're practically an orphan, you know," Petra said.

"I lived with *ata*, my grandfather."

"Yes, but, your mother…"

"Took her own life when I was eight," Maratse said. He fidgeted on the bench, looking at Petra as she slid closer and tucked her arm through the crook of his.

"It's cold," she said.

"*Iiji.*"

"Tell me about your mother. What was her name?"

"Piipaajik."

"What was she like?"

Maratse frowned for a moment, wondering if he should tell Petra about the last few days at the cabin, how he hadn't slept, and how it hadn't mattered, because he had been with his mother.

"She looked a lot like you," he said, after a few

minutes of silence.

"You mean to say she had long black hair and a pretty face, long legs, a brilliant mind..." Petra slapped her free hand on Maratse's arm as she laughed.

"*Iiji*," he said.

Petra caught the look on Maratse's face and stopped laughing. "What part?" she said.

Maratse shrugged, and said, "All of them."

They sat quietly on the bench, arms linked, through another ten or twenty sets of small waves choked with ice, as the tide came in, until Petra said it was time to leave. They drove in silence to the hospital. She took the lead when Maratse's silence continued from the car to the nurses' station. Petra did the talking. Maratse followed when the nurse led them to Mitti Petrussen's room.

"She won't respond," the nurse said. "But it's good to talk to her." She glanced at their uniforms, and said, "About general stuff, not questions."

"We understand," Petra said. She nodded her thanks when the nurse opened the door, and then took Maratse's hand, tugging him gently into the room.

Some of the strongest people in the world crack in the very moment they see a loved one in hospital, amazed at how they had been unaffected in all the days and nights prior to the visit, only to lose it the second they walk through the door.

Maratse was prepared.

He had confronted his demons already in the cabin by the river above the village of Ittoqqortoormiit. He had dealt with one death from his childhood, and then two more, projecting his mother beside him in some strange but satisfying self-coping strategy. He was stronger now and chose to leave Piipaajik on the east coast of

Greenland. He sat in the chair closest to Mitti's bed, studying the different tubes and equipment attached to her body, before nodding to Petra that he was okay.

"I'm just going to sit here for a bit," he said.

"I'll get some coffee."

"*Iiji*," Maratse said, tucking his hands into his jacket pockets and leaning back in the chair. He waited until Petra had left the room before he spoke, clearing his throat softly before he began. "I want to tell you something," he said, unaware that Petra had paused outside the room before shutting the door. It was open just enough so that she could hear him. "The nurse said it's good for you to hear people talk. So, I will tell you about Miliisa."

Petra leaned against the door frame as Maratse talked. Her breath caught in her throat as Maratse talked about his mother, describing Piipaajik for Mitti as if she was a character in a book. She smiled when he said she looked a lot like his friend *Piitalaat*, wondering if he knew she was listening, deciding that he didn't, but that she wouldn't go away just yet, maybe once he had finished his story.

Maratse described Ittoqqortoormiit as a wild place with wild weather. An extreme environment, "Perfect for growing up in. But difficult at times." He described his fall in the river, the shivering and shaking, and then Miliisa's body heat warming him, bringing him back to life. "My mother told me that I wasn't responsible," he said, as he neared the end of the story. "But we agreed that we each have a role to play. Miliisa is dead," he said. "My part in her story is over. But you're not dead, Mitti, and I still have a part to play in your story. So, I'm going to come here every day. I'll read some days, because I don't have many stories, at least not that I can tell, not properly. But I will talk to you. That will be my part. Your part is harder. You have to get better. That's the deal."

"She will," Petra said, as she opened the door. "But you don't have to come every day."

"Yes, I do," Maratse said.

"That's not what I meant. I meant we could take it in turns. If that's all right?"

Maratse nodded, turning in his seat to point in the direction of the nurses' station. "The nurse said it would help. I need to help."

"I understand," Petra said. "But it's getting late now. How about we come back tomorrow? There's someone else who needs help too."

"Smidt," Maratse said.

"Yes."

Petra waited for Maratse to walk to the door, pulling the door closed when he had said goodbye to Mitti. She took his hand as they walked along the corridor, and then stopped at the entrance to tug her smartphone from her pocket.

"I never did get coffee," she said. "I'll call ahead. Smidt can put the kettle on. We can bring cake."

Maratse smoked half a cigarette as Petra waited for Smidt to answer his phone. He flicked the butt into a bucket of sand as Petra gave up. She stuffed the phone into her pocket and pulled out the keys for the patrol car.

"We'll go, anyway," she said. "It's not far."

It wasn't far, but it was rush hour in Nuuk. While forty cars and a couple of buses would be considered light traffic anywhere else in the world, it was congested enough to slow them down. Petra stopped at a petrol station to buy a cake, and then handed it to Maratse as she drove. She parked in the lot reserved for the residents of the high-rise flat typically used for short-contract staff, and then told Maratse to hurry as a resident opened the door.

"So we don't have to buzz ourselves in," she said, smiling as a young man exited the building. He held the door until she reached it. Maratse carried the cake.

"Kuno lives on the fifth floor," Petra said, as she pressed the button for the elevator. She cast a guilty look at the stairs, and another one at the cake. "We won't tell Gaba," she said. "Agreed?"

"*Iiji*," Maratse said, following Petra into the elevator as the doors shushed open.

"The story you told Mitti," she said, once the doors were closed. "It's been bothering you, hasn't it?"

"For a long time."

"But you never speak of it."

"Which is why it's been bothering me." Maratse shrugged just as the elevator doors opened. They stepped out into the corridor, and he said, "But talking about it, staying at the cabin, it helped me come to terms with it. It helped me come to terms with what happened to Mitti, too." He followed Petra to Smidt's apartment.

"And now you can help her," Petra said. "That's good, David."

"*Iiji*."

Petra knocked on the door, looking at Maratse before calling out and knocking a second time. She tried the handle, turned it once and the door opened.

"It's heavy," she said, and then wrinkled her nose as warm air laced with something dark drifted through the gap between the door and the frame.

Maratse put the cake down and helped Petra open the door. It resisted, as if sandbags were piled against it on the other side.

"Kuno?" Petra said. She squeezed through the gap as soon as it was wide enough. "Kuno," she said again, louder.

It took Maratse another ten seconds to push the door open so that he could step into the apartment, but the heavy taint of death in the air told him just as much as the look on Petra's face; Kuno had not come to terms with what had happened to Mitti. But whatever part he had played in her story, it was now over.

Part 7

Since the collision at the roundabout on *Sipisaq Kangilleq*, Maratse had dealt with one death at a time. Constable Kuno Smidt's was the last one, at least that was what Maratse hoped. He pulled the folding knife from his utility belt, placed one foot between Smidt's legs and reached up to cut the cord looped around the young constable's neck. Petra called for an ambulance, followed by a second call to Greenland's Police Commissioner Lars Andersen.

"He wants to see us," she said, as she ended the call.

"Hmm," Maratse said.

He folded the knife back into the pouch on his belt and nodded for Petra to take Smidt's legs. They moved him away from the door. Maratse pointed at the couch in the living room further down the hall.

"No," Petra said. "I don't want to sit there. I want to stay with him."

Maratse nodded and tucked his hands into his jacket pockets. Petra clasped her smartphone, holding it to her side as she folded her arms across her chest.

"He's not much older than me," she said. "How well did you know him?"

"We worked together a few times – Upernavik and Qaanaaq," Maratse said. "He liked Greenland."

"He kept coming back," Petra said.

She started to say more but jumped at the sound of the intercom buzzing. She stepped around Smidt's body and buzzed the ambulance crew into the building. "Fifth floor," she said, before telling Maratse she would wait for them in the corridor.

Maratse stared at Smidt's face, wondering if the roles had been reversed, if *he* had been driving, not Smidt, would he have taken his own life? There was a history of suicide in Maratse's family, and an even longer history of suicide in Greenland. It was difficult to say if he had become hardened or accustomed to it. Either way, there was too much of it and the population was too small to sustain it, not without the psychological ramifications spreading through the people like the persistent roots of the crowberry bush.

"Crowberry," he whispered, as he thought about Piipaajik walking through the bushes, crumbling the imaginary asphalt into leaves. Regardless of the fact that Maratse knew that he had projected his mother into his own consciousness, that he had given her a form, clothes, speech even, he was still grateful. Without her to guide and shape his thoughts, it might have been *him* on the floor behind the door of *his* temporary lodgings.

"I don't believe that," Petra said, walking with Maratse into the lounge to give the paramedics space to work. "That look in your eyes, just when we came in. You were wondering if you would have done the same – taken your own life." Petra shook her head. "I don't think so, not even if you had been the one driving." She paused as the paramedics lifted Smidt onto the stretcher, continuing when they left the apartment. "You're one of the strongest people I know," she said.

"Smidt was strong."

"No," Petra said. "Not in the same way. You know what I'm talking about?"

Maratse shook his head. "I'm not sure I do."

"You carry the land with you," she said. "You are grounded. When you are in doubt, you return to the land for answers. That connection, the way you *connect* with your surroundings – it's what makes you human. It's what makes you *Inuk.*" She smiled when he frowned at her. "*Now* you must know what I mean."

"*Imaqa.*"

They heard the sound of the elevator doors closing, and then examined the apartment. There was no suicide note, no explanation of any kind. Smidt lived a simple orderly life, within which it was difficult to hide or disguise criminal intent. He died, most likely, at his own hands, something the autopsy would confirm. It would be entered into his records, and those records would follow his body, in a zinc-lined casket, home to Denmark. Petra nodded that she was done, and they left Smidt's apartment, locking the door behind them. Maratse picked up the cake, but Petra shook her head.

"No," she said. She pointed at the door of the rubbish chute in the wall, and Maratse dropped the cake inside it.

"You said the Commissioner wanted to see us?"

"I can go," Petra said. "If there's somewhere else you want to be?"

"*Iiji,*" Maratse said.

"I'll drop you at the hospital," Petra said, as she pressed the button for the elevator.

The nurses mentioned Maratse during the handover from the evening to the night shift at *Dronning Ingrid's*

Hospital. They agreed that he could stay, especially when his partner from that day now lay dead in the morgue. The door to Mitti Petrussen's room was open, and Maratse heard the evening shift leave, catching the last part of their conversation as they walked along the corridor to the end of the ward.

"…she *has* to recover now."

"To save him, she does. That's right."

Maratse fidgeted in the chair. He didn't know what was *right* or if he needed saving, only that Mitti was alive and needed to make a full recovery. Not for Smidt, not for Maratse, but for herself, for her future, and the future of her children – if she chose to have any. She would read about Smidt in the newspapers, but Petra's text from the Commissioner's office suggested that without a note, the reason for Smidt's death would never be anything more than speculation, and a sympathetic appeal to the local journalists would ensure it never became more than that.

A sharp beep from the machine monitoring Mitti caught Maratse by surprise, jolting his thoughts back into the room. He turned at the sound of the night staff soft-clacking into the room in their hospital clogs. Maratse stood up and moved his chair out of the way to give them space. He walked towards the door.

"You can stay, Constable," said the older of the two nurses. "She's coming around."

"Out of the coma?"

"Yes. A little earlier than anticipated, but that's a good sign." The nurse smiled. "Her body wants to come back."

Maratse moved to one side, curious to observe Mitti's recovery, the slow blink of her eyes, the deep furrows of confusion on her forehead, and the hand she raised to try and remove the tube from her nose. The nurse held her hand, gently but firmly, while her colleague talked to Mitti in Danish.

"Maybe she doesn't understand Danish," the older nurse said. "Constable?"

"*Iiji?*"

"Perhaps you could talk to her? In Greenlandic."

Maratse pulled his hands out of his jacket pockets and approached the end of Mitti's bed. He curled his fingers around the railing and looked at the nurse holding Mitti's hand.

"What should I say?"

"Tell her where she is. Tell her what happened. But first, Constable, you might tell her your name."

Maratse nodded. He looked at Mitti as she opened her left eye. He smiled, and said, "*Allu Mitti. Uanga Qilingatsaqi...*"

The End

Author's Note

_____

If you've read some of Maratse's earlier novellas, you will have already met Piipaajik and her younger sister Tannooq. If you haven't, you might enjoy *The Last Flight*, in which I explore a lot more of Maratse's background.

Inuk is a little more introspective than many of my other shorter works, but I hope you caught some of the cultural references along the way.

One last thought concerns the uncharacteristically loquacious Maratse – I don't think he's ever had quite so much dialogue as he has in *Inuk*, but then he did have a few things to work through. Time will tell just how chatty he becomes.

Chris
November 2019
Denmark

About the Author

Christoffer Petersen is the author's pen name. He lives in Denmark. Chris started writing stories about Greenland while teaching in Qaanaaq, the largest village in the very north of Greenland – the population peaked at 600 during the two years he lived there. Chris spent a total of seven years in Greenland, teaching in remote communities and at the Police Academy in the capital of Nuuk.

Chris continues to be inspired by the vast icy wilderness of the Arctic and his books have a common setting in the region, with a Scandinavian influence. He has also watched enough Bourne movies to no longer be surprised by the plot, but not enough to get bored.

You can find Chris in Denmark or online here:

www.christoffer-petersen.com

By the same Author

_____

THE GREENLAND CRIME SERIES
featuring Constable David Maratse
SEVEN GRAVES, ONE WINTER Book 1
BLOOD FLOE Book 2
WE SHALL BE MONSTERS Book 3

Novellas from the same series
KATABATIC
CONTAINER
TUPILAQ
THE LAST FLIGHT
THE HEART THAT WAS A WILD GARDEN
QIVITTOQ
THE THUNDER SPIRITS
ILULIAQ
SCRIMSHAW
ASIAQ
CAMP CENTURY
INUK
DARK CHRISTMAS
POISON BERRY
NORTHERN MAIL
SIKU

CHRISTOFFER PETERSEN

VIRUSI

STAND ALONE NOVELLAS
featuring Constable David Maratse
ARCTIC STATE

THE GREENLAND TRILOGY
featuring Konstabel Fenna Brongaard
THE ICE STAR Book 1
IN THE SHADOW OF THE MOUNTAIN Book 2
THE SHAMAN'S HOUSE Book 3

THE POLARPOL ACTION THRILLERS
featuring Sergeant Petra "Piitalaat" Jensen and more
NORTHERN LIGHT Book 1

THE DETECTIVE FREJA HANSEN SERIES
set in Denmark and Scotland
FELL RUNNER Introductory novella
BLACKOUT INGÉNUE

THE WILD CRIME SERIES
set in Denmark and Alaska
PAINT THE DEVIL Book 1
LOST IN THE WOODS Book 2

MADE IN DENMARK
short stories *featuring* Milla Moth set in Denmark
DANISH DESIGN Story 1

THE WHEELMAN SHORTS
short stories *featuring* Noah Lee set in Australia
PULP DRIVER Story 1

THE DARK ADVENT SERIES
featuring Police Commissioner Petra "Piitalaat" Jensen
set in Greenland
THE CALENDAR MAN Book 1
THE TWELFTH NIGHT Book 2

GREENLAND NOIR POETRY
featuring characters from Seven Graves, One Winter
GREENLAND NOIR Volume 1

ARCTIC ADVENTURE
featuring Captain Erroneous Smith
THE ICE CIRCUS

Made in the USA
Middletown, DE
18 December 2021

56520595R00154